PERTAK

KEVIN GAULT

Published by

Gault Ink

GaultInk.com

Cover Design by Les Solot
Logo Design by Steven Haught

DEDICATION

To my lovely, patient, and gracious wife.

CONTENTS

ACKNOWLEDGEMENTS

I would like to express my sincere gratitude to the many people who saw me through this book; to all those who provided support, talked things over, read, wrote, and assisted in the editing, proofreading, and design.

Above all I want to thank my wife, Cheryl, and my children, who supported and encouraged me in spite of all the time it took me away from them.

I would like to thank Luanne Hurst, Ph.D. for helping me in the processes of revision and editing.

Also, thanks to Timothy Fish, Trina Fish, Cheryl Gault, Becky Beall, Stephanie Gault, and Samuel Gault for their many contributions.

Finally, I would like to thank Ken Moody for his encouragement and help.

CHAPTER 1

The Encounter

The air was warm and breezy this evening with two of three suns shining high above. Liz was walking briskly toward the city cafe on the rocky, Jubian road where she was to meet Todd. She had a habit of tossing back her hair when she was nervous, and tonight she hadn't even thought about stopping herself. Since she'd been throwing out hints for some time now and Todd had finally asked her out, she wanted to make a good impression. Liz had gone home after work and dressed for her date but was now running late. She had been delayed because she kept having problems with her gravicar. One of the rear thrusters had lost communication with the vehicle's computer and was out of control, twisting back and forth. This made it almost impossible to steer. Having to stop twice at a service pod along the way had made her a half-hour late.

After making her way down to the cafe, she greeted the young man at the door. "Jimmy, have you seen Mr. Sevick?"

Looking at his reservation tablet, he replied, "No, Miss Paiste, but he called and left a message. He said he won't be able to join you tonight and that he'll call you later this evening; he also gave his apologies."

"He did, huh?" Liz sighed and gave him a frustrated look. *He probably even said it in that order too. That shows how much he thinks of me.* "Oh well, thanks, Jimmy; have a good evening." She popped him a credit chip as she walked out the door.

Jimmy smiled, thanked her, and scanned the credit chip to transfer the tip to his account.

It had begun to storm, just like an old Earth sandstorm before the enviro-systems built for the deserts were installed. Jubia was the last city on Pertak to install the system. Today, the system was down due to an overflow of Kidrasalie gas in the atmosphere. Walking back to where she had parked, Liz twisted the button on her sleeve and activated her personal shield, to avoid being hit by passing debris.

Liz made her way back to where she had left her brand new gravicar hovering and took the rising platform to her parking spot. She had purchased her vehicle just two days prior and had nothing but problems with it since. Upon her arrival, she noticed that the entire front end of her new Warp Two had been damaged in a hit and fly accident. She inspected the damage and just shook her head. "Not a note or anything...figures," she said. She climbed inside and headed home.

As she flew home, Liz had a hollow feeling in her stomach. She was hungry to be sure, but she felt that something else was wrong. Her home was a beautiful apartment in the southern suburb of Jubia. She parked, took the lift to the third floor, and walked to her door, where she lifted her hand to the metal impression beside the clear aluminite window and pressed lightly.

As she was walking into her apartment, her computer came to life: "How was your evening, Liz?"

"I don't want to talk about it!" As she spoke, Liz tossed her belongings onto her bed, "Windows at 0%."

At her command, the computer turned her windows completely dark. With three suns, Pertak never experienced true darkness. What on earth would have been called sunset light bathed the whole night in Jubia.

Liz shivered slightly and commanded, "Room temperature 78 degrees." No matter where she was, Liz was always cold, so she kept her own place a little warm.

Liz was a lovely human woman, about 5' 3" tall with long brunette hair and green eyes. Today was her birthday, and she had been looking forward to a meal and a show with Todd. She was hoping that he would surprise her with a piece of chocolate cake and a song from the workers at the cafe. After dealing with her gravicar, being stood up, then seeing her damaged vehicle, she had lost her appetite.

Slipping into her nightgown, Liz set her mind on her parents. They were on a working vacation in Telor, the largest city of the largest continent on the planet. Liz was thinking of how much she missed her parents and how she wished that she could just call them and cry on their shoulders.

Liz's parents had gone back to Telor to meet with a delegation of colonists who had settled on Pertak from

United Earth in 2325. They had lived there for almost 35 years just after marrying. She remembered her parents talking about the colonists settling on Gemia at one time, but a major meltdown of its polar caps made it uninhabitable, and they were evacuated. Liz's parents decided to settle on Pertak instead of choosing to return to United Earth.

Shaking her head, Liz brought herself out of her daydream. She looked to the stand by her bed and spoke to her vidcomm, "Messages?"

Her computer replied, "One message from your parents and one hang-up."

"Play the message from my parents and discard the other." She smiled as she spoke.

An image of her mother and father appeared on the screen. "Liz, dear, we called to wish you a happy birthday. We are sorry that we can't be there. You know we wouldn't miss your special day if this meeting were not very important. We'll fill you in on all the details when we return. Hope you had a great day. We love you!"

Liz decided to watch one of the many recorded productions that she had gathered over the years. She hoped that it, along with some snacks, would help her forget about her disastrous evening. When she finally turned over to go to sleep, her vidcomm beeped.

"It's probably Todd. After the night I've had, I certainly don't want to talk to him," she thought out loud. The comm beeped a second time. "Computer, mute that call!" Liz snapped.

"Call muted," said the computer. Whoever it was hung up and called back. Again, her comm beeped, then again and again.

Now annoyed, she threw her sheets off and answered with hostility. "Hello!"

The screen was dark, and the other voice was soft. "Miss Paiste, you have something that I need."

Squinting, she asked, "Who are you?"

"That's not important now. What is important, is that I must meet with you tonight." said the voice.

Liz insisted, "First, tell me who you are."

"I can't tell you over the comm, but it's very important that we meet tonight."

"No way, not tonight," Liz said. "I'm going to bed."

"Very well, I'll be in touch," said the voice. Liz stewed for a minute or two while complaining under her breath. She recognized the voice but couldn't quite remember. She dismissed the mystery and went to sleep. Almost immediately, Liz was awakened by a noise coming from her front room. At first, she tried to shrug it off. *Surely her computer would alert her to any break-ins.* But she kept hearing noises and knew for certain that someone or something was in the next room. Liz wrapped her housecoat around her, grabbed her enforcer, and slipped along the wall, being careful to stay in the dark. Apparently, she startled whoever was in the room because in the next instant, she saw a flash of light and felt the sharp cut of laser-fire hitting her chest. The intruder fired again, this time missing her altogether.

Too weak to move, Liz whispered, "Computer, call for help." The familiar acknowledgement of her command never came. She gasped, her knees buckled, and she fainted.

CHAPTER 2

GJED

The following morning was a beautiful spring-like day. Two suns were shining, and the sky was a deep pink color. Only a few pillow-shaped clouds dotted the sky. It promised to stay that way for at least a day or so.

Director Todd Sevick, a Pertakian male, was the leader of the enforcement department. He was a tall being of almost 6'5", and his face was very much like that of a human male with the exception of his slightly scaly appearance and his eyes. Every Pertakian male had two or three colors in each eye. These features gave them an almost reptilian look. Todd's eyes were green, blue, and a color that Pertakians called *zilla*. This color was like the United Earth color chartreuse, only more vivid. Todd called to explain to Liz what had happened the night before. (He had been called away for a top-secret emergency meeting).

To Todd's surprise, Liz's computer answered the call. "Please leave your message for Liz now, and she will return your call as soon as it is convenient for her to do so."

"Hi, Liz, this is Todd. I'm really sorry for what happened last night. My absence couldn't be avoided. Since you're not there, I guess I'll speak with you at the office…" Just as he was about to disconnect the call, Todd heard rustling over the line.

Liz's voice was weak and raspy. "Todd, help me! Someone broke into my apartment last night, and I've been shot."

Todd heard nothing for the next few moments. "Liz! Liz! Hold on! I'll be right there!" Todd slapped his vidcomm closed, disconnecting the call, and ran from his office.

About five minutes later, he arrived at Liz's apartment with a couple of enforcement department medibots and several officers. Todd pulled the lock-pick chip out of his pocket and placed it against the hand scanner. After a few moments, the wall opened for him. The team entered quickly and cautiously. Passing through her front room, they couldn't believe the destruction. Todd motioned for them to head for the bedroom.

Somehow, Liz had made it to her bed. A path in the debris showed where she had been. Liz tried to relay as much information about the break-in as she could before she passed out once again.

Todd pointed to the medibots and ordered, "You two, get her to a med-camp ASAP!" Watching her being carefully placed onto a levi-stretcher, Todd waited until they walked out the door.

As he took a closer look around, his mouth opened in awe. He just couldn't believe the destruction in a once highly organized apartment. *This is going to take some time.* He thought to himself.

The enforcement officers gathered all of the information available with their portable scanners. Todd ordered an enforcement field to be put up around the perimeter of the apartment. After they had completed their initial scans, he dismissed the officers while his four agents remained. Todd felt it necessary to regroup and to assess the situation in a more familiar and safe environment so he announced a meeting back at their headquarters. The five made their way back to GJED (Greater Jubia Enforcement Department).

***

The door placard read "Office of Director Todd Sevick." Agents Tim, Greg, Mike, and Trina entered and took their respective seats. Todd, now standing, walked from one side of the room to the other before speaking. He knew what they all were thinking, so he said it out loud, "Too many of our people have been taken out lately. You all know the problems we've been having...no hard evidence. I'm open for suggestions."

Tim spoke up first. "Does Liz even know what is going on around here?"

Todd answered, "She is only a secretary second class. You know I don't discuss cases with office personnel."

"Well, she is going to have to know something about it now," Tim stated.

Todd looked over at Greg and said, "I want you to go to that med-camp and see if you can get in to see her. If she is able to have visitors, find out what happened, and get all the information you can without going into detail about what we know.

Greg squinted as he spoke his mind: "Sir, with all due respect, shouldn't she be allowed to know that she could be in real danger?"

Todd replied, "I understand your sentiment, but it seems that we might already have a leak. I don't want to jeopardize the information and evidence we already do have by bringing untrained personnel into this."

Suddenly, Mike chimed in, "Did any of you notice that those medibots looked a bit different? The ones who took Liz out on the levi-stretcher had a different logo on their uniforms." The thought hung in the air for several seconds.

Trina said, "We usually work with GMC (General Med-Camp). Those bots were wearing uniforms that said *MMC*. Why would they be on this side of Jubia?"

Todd sighed in frustration and ordered, "Greg, check out Mercy Med-Camp, and see if she is there. The rest of you, take whatever equipment you need to make some sense of what happened last night and get back to Liz's apartment." Once the room was finally empty, Todd stared out of his clear aluminite window and wondered. He couldn't help thinking that if she died, he would be the one who would bear the blame.

***

Greg Herrod was a tall, thin human of 32 years with a light complexion, blonde hair, and green eyes. He decided to make his way to MMC using public transportation.

The repeltram was the fastest transportation known to the Jubians, and its route would take him directly to the med-camp. He looked around, found an empty seat, and sat down.

He was thinking about how careless they had been, not checking to make sure that the bots were from the appropriate med-camp. Greg was concerned that if they had lost Liz, they might never see her again. She was hurt pretty badly, and if she didn't get medical attention soon, she could die.

He couldn't bear the thought of another one of the GJED personnel being taken out. Besides, Greg knew how much the Director liked her. He'd been talking about their date for a week.

Once Greg arrived at MMC, he walked up to the front counter and inquired about whether Liz had been brought to the camp.

The bot at the front desk, who was made up to look like a Pertakian male, said, "I need your ID, sir." Greg pulled his ID card from his pocket and scanned it. He glanced over and looked through the semi-opaque aluminite wall to his left; he thought he saw the same med-transport that had taken Liz from her apartment. He recognized the vehicle from the thruster burns on the rear, indicating the use of deficient fuel.

When Greg saw the two medibots exiting, he thrust his ID card back into his pocket and sprinted toward the door. Once outside, he yelled, "Hey, stop!" One bot saw Greg running toward it and motioned to the other, which hurriedly closed the empty, rear cargo hatch. They both climbed inside the vehicle and took off quickly. Greg grabbed his enforcer, set it to maximum range, and fired. The first shot hit one of the rear thrusters, while the second shot took out the opposite front thruster, sending the gravicar into a wild spin. The pair of bots bailed out onto the rocky terrain below, and the vehicle crashed shortly after.

Greg headed down the hill to where they had bailed out. The bots were totally destroyed. He had wanted to catch them for interrogation, but instead, he now had more investigation to do. Greg located the datapacks on the bots, removed them, and shoved them into his pocket.

He tapped the communication device on his arm, reported the incident, and asked for a cleanup crew. Turning from the wreckage, Greg climbed the hill and once again entered the med-camp lobby. Apparently, the receptionist bot didn't have much of a short-term memory because it again asked him for his ID.

Greg rolled his eyes, pulled the card from his pocket, and scanned it again.

"What can I do for you sir?" asked the bot.

He asked about whether or not Liz had been admitted.

The bot informed him that no one matching her description had been admitted to the camp within the last 30 days.

Greg sighed, "I've spent half the morning here, and you've been no help at all!"

The bot with the painted-on smile said, "Thank you, sir; have a nice day!"

Greg headed back to GJED to try to decipher the datapacks taken from the medibots. On his trip back, he pulled the cards from his pocket and noticed that they had been badly burned. He thought to himself, *It'll be a miracle if I can retrieve anything from these cards.*

***

Back at headquarters, Greg told Todd about the trip and that Liz hadn't been admitted to the med-camp. He also told him that he had retrieved the datapacks from the medibots.

Todd sighed, thought for a moment, and looked back at Greg. "Just do the best you can to find her."

***

In Liz's apartment, Trina was doing an atmospheric print scan to find out what size being had been in the room with Liz. She had to be careful to take into consideration the officers that had been involved in the initial investigation, earlier that morning.

Mike Garend was a Pertakian male with medium-length black hair. His eyes were zilla, green, and orange. Mike had been giving Liz's computer a shakedown and was having to work around a very extravagant arrangement of separthims implanted into the memcards.

These separthims were encrypted containers that acted independently from the physical space of the memcard but were contained within for portability. They held the log information gathered from everything in the room. This information included things like vidcomm calls, atmospheric movement and pressure, temperature and lighting, and anything else that may have been recorded. The separthims should have detailed data regarding the conditions surrounding the intruder and the break-in.

One of the things that Liz had told them before she was taken was that her computer hadn't alerted her to the fact that an intruder was in her apartment though it seemed to behave normally in every other function.

Mike decided to test it out, so he looked at the food server and said, "Domarthian Estar Juice, chilled." A millisecond later, it began to appear. He picked up the glass and took a sip of the clear, brownish substance. Mike started gasping violently, grabbing at his heart and yelling, "AAAAHHHHH!" When the others looked at him, he added with a smile, "That sure went down smoothly. The food server seems to be OK."

GJED agents were used to breaking encrypted separthims mostly by using certain frequency variances provided by security companies. This did away with the necessity to actually have the answer to the challenge.

Tim lifted his resonator to the computer and ran a typical scan which included most of the known sequences, but for some reason the scan wasn't yielding any results. His native planet was named Cinessia. The members of his race were known for their intellects, and most of them were a medium to dark green color. He scratched his slightly tilted forehead and said, "This investigation is going nowhere. Mike, can you double-check this resonator?"

Trina's attempt to link GJED's computer to Liz's computer also wasn't having much success. In order to analyze anyone in the information gathered from the atmospheric print scan, she had to have the DNA count, size, weight, and mass of everyone known to have been in that room. This would leave the intruder as the only remaining being. She just didn't have the information needed in order to make that judgment by sight. There were too many beings to sort through, not to mention that Pertakian computers had a knack for counting humans as two beings because of the complexity of their skin tissue.

Trina walked through the torn-apart living room into the room where Tim and Mike were working. They were still attempting to break the first of several separthims. She asked, "Tim, can you tell me how I might link Liz's computer with the GJED computer? I've been trying to talk the computer into cooperating, but it's not going well. It just isn't responding."

Tim looked curious at her determined tone. "Try using the manual keyboard; we're just finishing with it now."

"Wow, haven't seen one of these in a while. Where'd she get it?" Trina looked respectfully back at Tim.

"It's an antique, dated all the way back to 21st century Earth. It looks like it came from the Japan sector."

Trina looked up at Tim with beautiful greyish-blue eyes and said, "Thank you."

Trina strained to remember the manual typing skills that she hadn't used since she was a little girl. Hitting the keys with increasing precision, she managed to get the computer to react to her commands.

Trying to shift Tim's focus off of Trina, Mike said, "Tim! Are you going to help me finish with this resonator or not?"

Tim smiled widely at Trina and said, "I wish you luck." Then he turned. "I'll be right there, Mike."

Mike's resonator was a new model that was long and cylindrical in shape and had a box at the bottom end with controls on it. Since the frequencies that they had used didn't seem to be working, Mike was asking Tim to provide him with some of the rarer frequency combinations. These combinations would be considered illegal if not being used by GJED agents.

Because of the order of the separthims, one had to break each in the order that they were formed. If one were broken out of sequence, the entire separthim lot along with the memory of the rest of the comm, would most likely be erased. Once Mike had retrieved the extended frequency combinations from Tim, he continued his scans.

***

Back at GJED, Greg was busy scanning and attempting to repair the damage done to the datapacks that he had taken from the two MMC medibots.

From what was recovered, the data on the memcards gave him the name of the bot manufacturer (DORWA) and their programmer (N'Lapeen). DORWA was a military weaponry and vehicles manufacturer. What was strange about this was that medibots were usually assembled by a corporation run by the Jubian government.

Greg was sitting at his desk in his corner office on the third floor overlooking a beautiful river that was a sparkling and radiant turquoise. Rubbing his temples, Greg looked disturbed. He lifted his head and said, "Computer, run all known information on DORWA. Please provide the owner's name, history, all dealings with bot technology, current operators of DORWA, and a complete history of N'Lapeen. Oh, and if N'Lapeen and DORWA have any dealings with each other, I want to know about it."

The computer hesitated for a second and replied, "Information not available. Further analysis of this subject matter is classified. Access is denied."

Confused, Greg inquired, "Computer, by whose order is this deemed classified?"

The computer came back instantly, "Unable to disclose that information."

"Why?" Greg asked, dumbfounded.

"The information requested is beyond your clearance level."

Greg tapped the communication device on his arm. "Greg Herrod to Director Sevick."

Todd answered, "Sevick here."

"Director, the computer has just informed me that my clearance isn't sufficient for a simple organization or personnel query. Do you know anything about this, Sir?"

Todd took a sip of his imported United Earth Asian tea. "What are you talking about?" he asked. "I certainly gave no such order, and the only person other than me who could give such an order would be the governor himself."

Greg thought for a brief moment. "Try your clearance and see what success you have."

Todd replied, "All right. I'll get back to you in a few moments."

Todd addressed the computer. "Give me access to files pertaining to N'Lapeen and DORWA."

The half machine, half female voice said, "Proceed."

"Have these two had any dealings with each other?"

The computer responded, "No correlation between N'Lapeen and DORWA exists."

OK, dead end, Todd said to himself. "Who gave the order to limit Gregory Herrod's computer access?"

"Governor Blok was responsible for the order," replied the computer.

Todd said, "Computer, set up an appointment for me with the Governor as soon as possible."

He sat back in his chair and thought for a moment, then tapped the communication device on his arm, "Agents Fraish, Herrod, Renard, and Garend, report back to my office as soon as possible."

Tim responded, "We will be on our way in five minutes."

Greg followed, "On my way sir."

CHAPTER 3

The Debriefing

A meticulously dressed Pertakian male was questioning two others about what had taken place the previous morning, "Well, what did you find?"

"Nothing much, sir," said Fenoc. "We did find a memcard belonging to the young lady, but as of yet we haven't been able to get any data off of it."

"And the girl?" asked the man impatiently.

Fenoc replied with a bit of apprehension, "We're still working on that, but I can tell you that the plan went off without any problems whatsoever."

"Good, keep working on that chip; we've got to find out where it is." He started toward the door.

Fenoc had an idea. "Sir, I think Tork and I ought to go through the stuff again just to make sure nothing was overlooked."

"Useless!" the Pertakian exclaimed. "I'm certain by now that GJED are there and have everything sealed. Do as you're told and get to work!" Exiting the room, he muttered about workers who don't listen and think too much.

Tork gave a mutinous look to his partner, Fenoc, and said, "Let's head back and go through the stuff again. You heard the same speech I did regarding patriotism and our duty to carry out our mission regardless of the consequences. We'll be heroes when we find it and deliver it ourselves."

Fenoc responded, "Tork, are you sure that your heart can handle another one of these tense situations?"

Tork, somewhat frustrated, said, "Just c'mon. I'm fine."

Fenoc nodded, and the two slipped out the door into the gravicar parked outside, and headed toward Liz's apartment.

***

The group gathered together in Todd's office and were seated. Todd began the meeting by asking each in turn what information had been gathered. Explaining the problem with Greg's computer clearance, he told them that he had made an appointment with the Governor. He asked the team if they had any other inquiries for his upcoming meeting.

Mike spoke up, "I would like to know how a secretary, second class, has enough computer knowledge to set up such an elaborate system for personal use. Why does she need that much security?"

"Point noted, Mr. Garend," Todd said while scratching his chin.

Mike stood to his feet, slicked back his glistening black hair, and walked toward the door. "I'm going to check with her co-workers to find out any information on her personally," he said.

While the meeting was going on in the director's office, Yalan, a young Pertakian female who was temporarily replacing Liz in her duties as secretary, second class, had just finished putting everything on her new desk in its proper place. Noticing some memcards that were a shade darker than the rest, she reached over, slid one into her computer, and said, "Scan for subject matter." A screen full of icons showed up with no titles. "Open one of the folders, please," said Yalan.

The computer replied, "Specify, please."

"Let's go with the top, left corner one."

The computer replied, "This folder has been encrypted. In order to gain access, the proper name for this folder must be provided."

Just out of curiosity, she commanded, "Override!" The folder opened and displayed a page of jumbled numbers. She tried another, and it contained a page of jumbled letters. Each of the other files contained one or the other but certainly didn't make any sense. Yalan pulled the card from her computer and put in another of the odd-colored cards, just to discover the same thing. She checked the regular-colored cards for information, and they yielded case files as they should. She wondered about the darker colored cards but soon dismissed them from her mind.

***

After the meeting was over, Todd went home and tried to relax but found it nearly impossible. He decided to go to his favorite thinking spot, the canyons. Just the trip alone was worth the effort.

Leaving his apartment, he took a scenic route which included flying lower than the rest of the traffic which in itself was always an adventure. As he approached the many canyons, he headed toward his favorite spot.

Todd climbed out of his vehicle and felt the heaviness of the air and the suns beating hot upon him. He ducked into a cave where he could be alone and just think. Todd pulled a candle from his pocket and lit it, and set it on the Memit rocks beside him.

He began to read an old book that his father had given him. His father was one of the founders of Jubia, back before it was the thriving city that it had now become. It felt good to be away from the pressures of work, yet he couldn't keep his mind from wandering back to Liz. The chill of the sunless cave was refreshing and made him feel as if he were on United Earth at night. Todd missed that feeling; though he had visited only once, he was hooked. He hoped that one day he would be transferred there, but didn't dwell on the idea.

After a few hours, Todd decided to head home. His sleep that night was troubled, and he awoke the next morning very tired as if he hadn't slept at all. "Back to work," he muttered.

***

"Security breach! Security breach! Leave the area immediately!" The enforcement's security perimeter announced. Fenoc looked at Tork in horror. Just when they thought they had fooled the security sensors and had entered, the computer knew it and announced it—loudly—to the entire building. They knew that the enforcement team would soon be arriving, and they couldn't be caught, not now. "Don't touch anything; this whole area must be monitored," whispered Fenoc.

Tork nodded, "Let's get out of here, quick!"

Running down the hall, the two encountered a couple of apartment complex security bots with paralyzers drawn. Having no time to slow down, the pair rolled, giving the bots hardly any time to react. As paralyzers were fired, they slammed into the bots, knocking them over. In the next instant, the bots fired on the two at point-blank range, killing Tork and barely just missing Fenoc. Fenoc fled the building hoping to get a clean getaway but was in such a panic, he couldn't think straight.

Trina, returning to continue her work in Liz's apartment, saw the Pertakian running toward her and gave him a very strange look. Fenoc flew by her at a speed she couldn't believe and headed directly toward his gravicar. She saw the bots headed down the hall toward her and decided that she'd better have a second look. Though she couldn't get a good look at his face, she was able to get the vehicle's ID as it flew off. It took off so fast that it ran into two other gravicars before getting out of the lot and ducking out of sight to avoid further recognition.

Trina stepped inside the apartment building only to see a young Pertakian male lying on the floor. After a brief examination, she saw that he'd been shot at close range and killed.

She realized a sound was coming from inside his colorful jacket. Bending over to listen, she heard a Pertakian countdown, "Jloven, Bzet, Flendo, Bork." Trina knew she only had a few ticks left to do something about it, so she twisted on his personal shield which lifted him off the ground. She grabbed him by the collar and flung him out the door. BLAM!

The metallic explosion was fantastic and resonated throughout the parking facility! Trina screamed in reaction, and tears welled up in her eyes. *Pull yourself together, Trina,* she thought to herself.

Tapping the communication device on her arm, she said, "Director Sevick, this is Trina."

Todd poked at his communicator and said, "Sevick Here."

Trina said in her now-composed voice, "Director, there's been a break-in at Liz's apartment. One of the two suspects was shot, killed, and just self-destructed. The other fled the scene."

Todd's first reaction was, "Has anything been disturbed at the apartment?"

"I don't know, sir. I had just arrived," said Trina.

"Keep me posted. Let me know if you find out anything on who these guys were," Todd replied.

Trina volunteered, "I was able to get the number off the fleeing gravicar."

"Good work! Give it to me and I'll have it checked out."

Trina signed off and walked down the hall to Liz's apartment to check out the damage. It looked as if they had only just broken through the force field, got frightened, and attempted to leave the scene. She asked herself, "Who would be bold enough to break-in after an investigation has already been started?"

***

Mike walked into Todd's office with a sly grin on his face.

Todd asked, "What's going on?"

"I'm here," Mike remarked.

"Why so chipper, Mike?"

Mike was very happy to tell Todd the good news. "Oh, I've just had a fantastic morning. I got a date with the new girl, Yalan. I can't believe how beautiful she is. Her golden hair, murky eyes, and phenomenal figure are more than anyone could ask for."

Todd grabbed a glass and said, "Have some warm nectar; it'll get you going."

Mike waved his hand. "Thanks just the same, but I've already had my morning food."

Tim, sitting across the room, asked Mike about what his investigation had yielded.

Mike thought a moment. "Well, in a word, *Nactev*." This was Pertakian for "Nothing." Mike continued, "It seems that the only two girls who even knew Liz at work really had no personal relationship with her. It looks like she had no real friends, at least here in Jubia."

Todd changed the subject. "I had my appointment with the Governor. It seems that a computer security breach had taken place, and an attack on some of Greg's personal files had been attempted. The demotion was a temporary measure until the damage could be assessed and rectified. At this very minute, the issue is being corrected. So, Greg, you'll be back in business soon. Tim, Mike, please join Trina at Liz's apartment and try to break through some of those separthims.

"We'll give you a buzz when we find something," said Tim.

Todd replied, "Be sure that you do!"

Greg walked back into his office, sat down in his chair, and looked up at the ceiling. A slight grin came over his face as he commanded, "Computer, now tell me about N'Lapeen and DORWA. I want all information previously requested! Now we'll finally start to unwrap this situation."

Greg waited and waited and finally the computer responded, "DORWA is an organization owned and operated by a parent company by the name of Ontra which is directed by shareholders which in turn appoint a head that has limited power. DORWA manufactures military equipment for the Jubian government, specifically inter-atmosphere warships. DORWA has been dormant for several years because of the peace talks between the powers. Board members include Peutkov, Jazt, Oinst..."

"Computer desist! Tell me more about recent ventures of the company and if they have engaged in any robotic activity in the past, say, 35 years," Greg insisted.

"Searching for data. No robotic endeavors have been supported by DORWA," stated the computer.

Greg thought for a moment, and inquired, "What does DORWA do now?"

The computer replied, "DORWA is currently producing limited edition vehicles for an unknown clientele."

Greg wiped his mouth with a downward motion, thinking, "Send all background information on N'Lapeen to my gravicar. I'll retrieve it there."

***

Trina yelped as she jumped up and said, "I think I finally found a way to connect Liz's computer with the one at GJED. I'm going to try to remote in now.

Tim heard her and in a moment of panic yelled, "Trina, no! If you remote in now, you run the risk of breaching the rest of the separthims and destroying the data in the comm." Trina was confused and a just a little perturbed. She thought that Tim had understood what she was attempting to do.

Tim looked over at Mike and asked, "How is the process coming?"

Mike replied, "I need to show you something. Come over here, you too, Trina." The two walked together through the living room and entered the closet that held the computer.

A bit earlier in a fit of frustration, Mike had made the closet a bit larger by pulling out his particle destabilizer and disintegrating the wall.

Mike exclaimed, "Look at this!" He pointed to the screen. "When I located the first separthim within the memcard, the computer came to life and showed me a screen full of jumbled numbers and letters. It seems to be a code of some kind, blocking our way to the other separthims."

Tim said, "I congratulate you on your discovery. Where do we go from here?" Trina looked up at Tim, and he looked back and smiled.

Mike gave Tim a smirk. "I thought you might have some ideas given that enormous brain of yours."

Tim replied, "The density of my brain does not make it any larger than yours. It only makes it easier to amass information, retain, and retrieve it."

Trina sensed that Mike might attempt to carry this conversation a little too far and spoke up, "You two carry on like children. Mike, I'm sure Tim was only joking. We'll do anything we can to help."

Mike, not looking at Tim just yet, said, "Trina, can you run this data to see if there is a pattern, perhaps a correlation between any known language or phraseology having to do with Liz's life?"

Tim looked at Trina, and back at Mike. "We will get right on it."

"Not so fast, Brainy, you're going to help me find the order of the remaining separthims."

Schwaa—the wall disappeared, and Todd walked into Liz's apartment. "The mess left by our intruders is being cleaned up outside. I'd like to know exactly what happened out there. By the way, Trina, that gravicar number was a dead-end. It was a new vehicle that was never registered. It was stolen from a lot just down the street from GJED and recovered shortly after."

Todd went over to Mike and began looking over his shoulder. "It looks like you've got quite a job on your hands."

Mike muttered, "Should be easy. I've broken through hundreds of these things, but for the life of me, I've never seen anyone organize separthims so erratically."

CHAPTER 4

The Blavs

Greg maneuvered his gravicar toward the Blavs, a part of town that was industrialized and dumpy. The area was known for an algae-like fungus that was a dingy pinkish-grey color and covered just about everything. He was looking for the building described by the computer and had to do it the hard way since satellite tracking didn't work in this area of town.

He was trying to locate a man by the name of Rentash, a lead given to him by the computer under the subject of N'Lapeen. Greg had attempted without success to use his infrascanner to see how many beings there were in the building of interest. He looked down and spotted the building that appeared to be the correct one, so he landed his craft and proceeded inside.

He started by walking to the back of the building where his scanner showed a man who appeared to be close in age to Rentash. "Mr. Rentash," he yelled, "Are you here? I need to speak with you, sir." Greg rounded the corner and appeared in the next room. "Mr.

Rentash?" He heard a whirring sound and tried to duck as a piece of 150lb Zefermite was hurled toward him by a machine in the room. The block of metal hit him on his right side as he was angling to get out of the way and knocked him over. Greg pulled his enforcer out of its pouch, not even waiting for the heads-up display to show a target lock, and fired at the fleeting shadow heading toward the next room. He pulled himself from the floor, gathered his senses, and went after the person he saw running. "Hey! Who are you?" Greg demanded.

Looking left and down the hall, he saw a man who looked to be a young Pertakian with a red mark that covered the entire left side of his face. "Hey!" Greg yelled. The Pertakian disappeared into the street. Greg gave chase but couldn't tell where he went. Two men appeared behind him and jabbed him in the ribs with something sharp.

"Don't move!" the man ordered. Greg stood still as one of the men took his enforcer. In the next instant, he felt some discomfort as a device injected a substance into his bloodstream which put him to sleep.

***

Mike arrived home just in time to get dressed and pick up his date, Yalan. He was taking her for a night on the town. He couldn't wait to show her what he had planned.

Trying to recognize which domicile was hers, he noticed that the foliage on the wall that composed the structure was in the shape of the Jubian flag. The flag showed a city-like silhouette with a small shuttle full of majomite, the main export of the city.

He maneuvered his vehicle next to the side of the structure where Yalan was to be waiting for him. When he didn't see her, he called her on her vidcomm.

Yalan answered, "Oh, hi, Mike. I'll be right out."

"I'll be waiting just outside," Mike assured her, trying not to sound anxious.

Within a few minutes, Yalan stepped out onto the speedwalk headed toward the waiting lot. As he saw her coming, he hopped out and hurried over to greet her.

"Hi! Right this way, ma'am." Yalan grabbed his arm, and Mike walked her to the car, manually opening the passenger door for her. She stepped into his vehicle, and he closed her door with the same gentleness that he had used to open it. As he was walking around the car to get in the driver's seat, he let out a boyish, "Whoo!"

Once inside, he looked over at her and asked, "What kind of music do you enjoy?"

Yalan smiled, "I like ancient earth music. You know, stuff like Bach, Beethoven—classic music, they called it."

Mike thought out loud, "The closest I can come to that would be Gemian group music."

"Sounds good," Yalan nodded.

Mike looked over at her golden hair in the sunlight, which brought out a small greenish tint that complimented her pale and faintly scale-like skin. He caught himself staring, straightened in his seat, and took off. Mike listened as Yalan gently hummed along to the catchy music as they made their way to Jubia's Stabian Center.

The Stabian Center was named after Bervus Stabian, a famous actor who was trained in the San Francisco sector of United Earth. Stabian was said to have rivaled the very best actors Earth had to offer.

They arrived at the door just a little early in order to be assured of the location that was reserved for them. They sat on a deck that immediately lifted upward and placed them close to the center of the dome with a perfect view of the show.

The play was a modern one with costumes to match. The main character was a thief who was actually a Pertakian male made up to look like a human. At the end of the play, the criminal was caught because of his carelessness in putting on his disguise and sentenced to life in duty camp. As the players came out and took their bows, the two applauded loudly.

Yalan looked at Mike with appreciation. "That was very well done," she exclaimed.

"I really enjoyed it too," Mike concurred. "Would you like to go to a little cafe in the Caverns?"

Yalan smiled, "Yes, that sounds good."

At the cafe, Mike found himself staring at Yalan again. With a puzzled look, she inquired, "Is there something wrong?"

"What?" Mike asked, coming out of his daze. "No, no, nothing's wrong. I was just thinking."

"Thinking about what?" she asked.

"It's this case that I'm on. I'm not getting anywhere, and I just can't get my mind off of it."

Yalan sounded interested. "Can you talk about it?"

He shook his head, then added, "Well, as long as I don't mention specifics, I suppose I can tell you about it in general."

Mike told her that a person had been shot and kidnapped. He mentioned how knowledgeable this person was with technology and the advanced security techniques used in this person's apartment.

Yalan replied, "That sounds like the girl that had my job before me. I heard she was very good with that sort of thing too."

Mike said, "That's right; I forgot that you're the one who's temporarily filling Liz Paiste's position."

"Yes, is that who you're talking about?" asked Yalan.

Mike caught himself. "Well...let's just say... Hey, have you heard any good gossip or anything else about Liz?"

Yalan grinned because she knew she was onto him. "I heard that she was beautiful, had a date with the boss, and that she kept to herself a lot."

Mike smiled too because he knew he had given away too much, "Has there been anything unusual about her office, her desk, or the way she kept things?"

Yalan thought back to her first day. "She did have an unusual way of filing her supplies."

Mike, sorry that he had started talking about work, said, "I'd better let it rest for now; I'm sure that I'm boring you."

As they were talking, a very large Pertakian female with imposing features walked up and asked, "Are you two doing all right? Can I get you anything else?"

Yalan lifted her head and said, "Another Earth spring water, please. It is so sweet compared to Pertak's water. I almost feel like I'm going to gain weight drinking it."

Mike agreed, "Make that two. Thank you."

The two talked about trivial things for a little while longer, finished their drinks, and started to walk out to Mike's gravicar. The large Pertakian server watched curiously as Mike and Yalan left. As soon as they had passed her, she got up and walked quickly to the back of the cafe.

Walking Yalan to her door, Mike was hoping that she would say something positive about the evening.

Yalan looked fondly into Mike's eyes and said, "Thanks so much for everything. I can't remember when I've had so much fun. Can we go out again sometime?"

Mike, now grinning from ear to ear, stumbled to get the words out. "Well, I am uh, really, um, glad. Can I call you?"

"Anytime! Please do," replied Yalan.

Mike, still not believing what he had just heard, said, "Goodnight, Yalan."

"Goodnight, Mike, sleep well."

He stood and watched as she used her entry card. Safely inside, she waved to Mike as the door closed.

Half yelping out loud, he just about ran down the speedwalk back to his vehicle, hopped in, and headed home.

***

Greg awakened to a tapping sound. It sounded like a stone hitting an aluminite window over and over again. Greg struggled but was inhibited by something. He felt like he was in a very small room or maybe even a box.

He opened his eyes, but everything seemed fuzzy. He tried hard to see what was encasing him but couldn't make out anything. Touching the wall in front of him, he felt the electric fuzz of a force field over ribs of some sort of building material.

Greg knew exactly how these fields worked since he had once designed and built these types of enclosures. It would be very easy for him to defeat the system if only he could see. He still felt woozy from the drug that had put him to sleep, so squinting did very little to help him see. The difference between this enclosure and the ones that he had built was that this one had him in a prone position facing up.

Greg pressed against the field. He knew that a certain amount of pain would come as he pressed harder. Instead of pain, the barrier began to feel more solid, and he heard a sizzling sound. Greg was puzzled at first, but then he heard footsteps as someone entered the room. He realized that the sizzling sound wasn't coming from his enclosure but from a hydraulic door.

A metallic voice greeted him. "Mr. Herrod, how are you feeling?"

Greg straightened and said, "Who are you, and why are you holding me here?"

"Come now!" The voice now sounded more human. "Are you comfortable?"

"What do you think?" he snapped.

The voice climbed in pitch. "I think you'd better be glad that you're alive."

"What did you do to me? he demanded. I can't see!"

The voice was calm and clear. "Your condition is only temporary. I assure you that you'll be fine in a couple of hours. Just be patient."

Greg smacked the force field with his fist. "And what is this? I've never felt a field that didn't give proportional pain to resistance."

"You're in a containment cell, not a torture cell. Please relax and make yourself at home. Would you like to stand?"

Greg nodded, and the human voice commanded, "Computer, containment cell vertical." The box seemed to levitate and turn on its own.

Once standing, Greg prepared himself for the jolt to come and forced himself against the field with all of his might, but to no avail. He tried multiple times with no result but fatigue.

The voice laughed, "There is no reason for violence. Just wait for a few days, and we'll let you out."

"A few days?" Greg, suddenly feeling claustrophobic, went into a rage. "What right do you have to keep me here at all?" he demanded.

"Mr. Herrod, as far as we're concerned, you don't have any rights on this world."

Greg stood still and thought to himself, *Who is "we"? Why do they use a bot to talk to me?* He insisted, "Let me talk to your superior!"

"I am all you need for now," said the voice.

CHAPTER 5

A Breakthrough

Early the next day, Todd was surprised when Greg failed to attend the morning meeting. He kept buzzing Greg's communication device every few minutes but received no reply. He thought out loud, "It isn't like Greg to stand me up without at least contacting me."

Beep...beep...beep, Tim's communication device chimed. He pressed the button on his sleeve. "Fraish here."

Todd inquired, "Tim, have you heard from Greg this morning?"

Tim responded, "No, I have not had a chance to check in with him."

"I can't seem to reach him," said Todd.

"He probably just had a late night and is not wearing his comm. I will check on him. Fraish out."

Mike, looking over at Tim, said, "Go ahead. I can take care of things here for a while. Oh, and I've already gotten something back from the main labs about the jumbled letters and numbers. Listen to this before you go, so you can think about it on the way to Greg's place. The phrase 'set article match' kept coming up. It was found 11 times within the items that we tested."

Tim looked thoughtful and exclaimed, "If I remember correctly, that is 21st century English used by citizens of ancient Earth. Start your research there."

Mike replied, "All right, I will.

"OK, see you later. Oh, and Trina is going to come over soon to set up the imagizer again to take a second atmospheric print. She thinks she has found a way to pipe the information into the GJED computer via her comm." Tim opened the wall and headed out.

Mike muttered to himself, "We could actually get this job done if we all just stayed here and finished up. It's been taking entirely too long. Every time we make headway, something..."

Mike heard a pleasant hum coming from the next room. Trina walked in with a smile on her face. "Hi, Mike. How are you doing this fine day?"

Mike smiled back, "Fantastic! I had a great night, last night."

"I'm so glad." "Have you seen Tim this morning?"

"He walked out the door, just before you showed up. He went to see if he could find Greg, who apparently didn't show for his meeting with Todd this morning. He should be back soon if he finds Greg quickly enough."

"OK, can you give me a hand with this imagizer? I need to get it calibrated with my comm."

***

Since the city of Jubia was so crowded, most beings lived in apartment-like dwellings. Greg lived in an outlying area in his own residence. On United Earth, it would be called a house, but on Pertak it was called a sanda. As Tim neared Greg's sanda, he saw that the clear aluminite windows had been set at 40 percent, and no one was around.

Tim parked his gravicar in front of Greg's residence and headed to the back in an attempt to see inside. Once behind the sanda, he could see directly into the sleeping area and could tell that the bed was made and that nothing looked disturbed. Tim touched the call button on the door panel and was greeted with a recorded greeting asking him to leave a message.

Perplexed, Tim walked around the other side of the sanda and noticed that Greg's gravicar was gone. He tapped the communication device on his arm to check in with Todd. Todd wondered why Greg hadn't communicated his plans. He instructed Tim to go back to Liz's apartment, but to call some of Greg's friends on the way to find out if they knew anything.

Trina was just finishing the link-up to the GJED computer using her personal comm. Thanks to Mike's quick thinking, a disastrous result was averted. When the link was activated, it caused a particle disruption which would've destroyed the atmospheric prints. Mike heard the whine of the imagizer slowing down to reverse itself. He grabbed the device and turned it off, stopping it before it did any damage. Now, the only thing left was to persuade the imagizer to take the prints needed to send to GJED.

Tim scanned his ID card at GJED's security kiosk and stepped inside. As he entered, Trina smiled widely, "Hi, Tim! How are you today?" As the imagizer was making a print, she instructed Tim and Mike not to move.

Since the imagizer could not analyze the information itself, the link-up was necessary to process the data. The computer relayed information back to Mike's comm as the analysis progressed. The hope was, as before, that after discounting everyone involved with GJED and the medibots, only those not known by the GJED computer would show up. These images should be those of the intruder(s). When the imagizer obtained unusually good scans, GJED's computer was sometimes able to make out faces with some detail. After the scan had finished the room where Tim and Mike were standing, Trina told them that they could get back to work.

Back at GJED, Todd was meeting with Petolis, a Domarthian solacemar, regarding the visit Todd and the governor were planning. As they both stood and walked toward the door, Todd nodded at Petolis and said, "I am looking forward to our next meeting, Petolis. I do hope we can work together on this."

Petolis responded, "May evil flee from you, my friend."

Todd tipped his head slightly. "May evil flee from you, my friend." The two parted company.

Immediately, Todd tapped the communication device on his arm and said, "Sevick to Garend."

Mike answered, "Garend here. What can I do for you?"

"Mike, I'm going to stop by and see what kind of progress you are making with the imagizer. I'll be there in a few minutes."

Todd had missed Liz's smiling face every day as he walked past her desk. As he passed her desk today, Yalan, who hadn't even acknowledged him in days past, greeted Todd, wishing him a good day. *Well, maybe today will be a bit different from the others,* he thought to himself. First, he had a good meeting with the solacemar, then a smile from the new secretary.

Todd walked out of the building with a new sense of optimism and headed straight toward his gravicar. Traveling at speed, he could reach Liz's apartment in only two or three minutes.

Once there, Todd scanned his ID card and was allowed inside. Finding the crew in the back room, he jokingly said, "Don't you people ever work around here?" The three of them just stood there looking at him.

Tim spoke first. "No, we were actually thinking about how long it has been since we have seen you in such a good mood."

Todd inquired, "Well, what's the news?"

Trina looked sort of dejected. "So far, nothing. It's as if no intruder had been in this room. The scan hasn't finished yet; we've got about 15 minutes to go before we're through, then the time it takes to analyze the data."

"Let me know the minute that you hear something back from GJED's computer," said Todd. "Now, I want to have a look at those separthim encryption codes. I would like to try to decode them myself. Tim told me about the ancient Earth reference, and I have an idea."

Tim offered, "Right this way, Director!" and led him to the computer.

About twenty minutes later, the print was finished, and the data finally started coming in. Trina had just started looking over the discouraging data when Liz's vidcomm buzzed once and then again. Tim motioned at Mike. "Please try to trace this call."

"Screen on." He answered, "Hello?"

A cautious voice replied, "Is Liz there, please?"

Tim scratched his head and looked at Trina curiously. He answered, "No, she is not available. Can I take a message for her?"

"Sure—but who is this?" asked the voice.

"This is Agent Fraish," he replied.

"Hi, Agent. I'm Liz's mother, Maria. I've been trying to get in touch with her. Is there something wrong?"

"We have been attempting to contact you and your husband for the last few days. It seems you have been away." Tim took the next few minutes to tell the whole story as delicately as he could.

After the call ended, Tim discussed the conversation with Trina. Mike had been listening while recording the conversation. "I hated to tell her that, so far, we have no solid leads regarding the disappearance of her daughter," noted Tim.

Mike piped up, "As soon as Todd breaks the code for that first separthim, we'll be in business, hopefully."

Tim walked back to the small computer room and asked Todd what the phrase "set article match" meant.

Todd tilted his head slightly. "That's what I've been trying to remember. I think it's a phrase from an old Earth play, but it's kind of vague to me, and I can't really recall the circumstances.

Todd decided to take a break to think over the situation, so he left the apartment. As he was walking, he tapped the communication device on his arm and spoke to the computer at GJED. He asked it to scan any ancient Earth data for the phrase "set article match." He was certain that it had something to do with a performance of some sort, so he asked the computer to specifically concentrate on those types of records.

Within a few minutes, Todd received a reply. It was just as he had thought; an ancient Earth comedy had used the words "set article match" eleven times. It was in reference to an English professor speaking to a computer programmer. The programmer could not spell properly, and his code would error out. The message that popped up on the screen said, "indeed." This made Todd chuckle. He bounded inside the apartment and trotted toward the back room. "I've got it! I know the code!" he exclaimed. He spoke: "Computer, respond to this keyword: indeed."

The computer responded, "Access granted; please proceed."

CHAPTER 6

Misdirection

Click, click, click—the fingers of the bot thumped on the metallic table in an orderly fashion, as if it were bored with what it was doing. *I can't stand that noise!* Greg thought so loudly that his words should have been heard. *I wish they wouldn't make them so life-like. It's almost a mockery of the race. At least I can almost see normally now.*

Feeling the wall behind him, he tried to find a seam or anything irregular. Knowing that the bot would fix its gaze on him if he called attention to himself, he worked quietly and carefully. Greg rubbed his fingers up and down, until he finally found a slight difference in height on the wall of the box. He determined that the wall was made of ufinar, a kind of fiber that was usually very strong but if breached, could be easily broken. The only problem was that it let out a very high pitched noise if bent or broken, so this was not going to be easy.

Click, click, click...the bot was tapping even faster now, as if it were about to make a decision to do something. "Hey, metal head!" Greg shouted. "Can't you do anything but annoy me? I can't stand to hear that clicking sound! Why don't you sing or something? Anything but that maddening tapping of your fingers!"

The bot turned its head and looked at him. It didn't say a word, just tapped its fingers a bit more slowly.

Greg, still working to get a grip on the seam that was basically his only means of escape, had gotten hold with the index finger of his right hand. He carefully pulled it toward him trying to get another finger in the crack. *Ouch!* he yelled inside his head. The harder he pulled, the more the gap tightened, pinching his finger. *That's odd. I can't seem to find a way to make it give. It's as if it had reversed resistance, but that's impossible. I created this substance; it took me two years to perfect it. How did this tin-head get this material? This stuff is top secret.*

The bot stood, walked over to the door, and looked straight up. It lifted its arm and out of its forefinger came an instrument that shot a beam of light at the ceiling above. A section of the ceiling moved away, and a small box was lowered automatically. The bot opened the box which revealed what appeared to be a memcard catalog. It inserted a memcard into the box and retrieved another. The bot lifted its arm again and shot a light at the ceiling above, causing the machine to move back into the ceiling and the section of ceiling to be replaced. It turned and walked to the far side of the room behind where Greg's box was standing. He was facing away from the bot, so he was unable to see what it was doing. He heard a swoosh, a clunk, and another swoosh. Greg figured that he had put the memcard into some sort of storage bin, since the swoosh wasn't loud enough to be a door.

Greg struggled to get a glimpse of the bot but couldn't see anything beyond the limited view permitted by his enclosure. He heard the bot coming back, so he straightened to his original position and asked, "What was that thing you deposited?"

The bot replied, "I am not disclosing any information to you, human. Your termination is close at hand. Is there anything that you require?"

He answered, "Sure, I require that you let me go."

"That's not within my ability. Is there anything else?" asked the bot.

Greg had an incredible idea, "OK, yes. Play some music for me, very loudly."

The bot asked, "Would you have any selection in mind?"

"As a matter of fact, yes. Play 'Dep Elexpi' from the Galkin era on Mars, 2157. Play it very loudly!"

There was a slight hesitation from the bot; then the music started to play. The music started out softly but soon filled the room with sharp squeals and extremely low booming bass. The music was so loud that any prolonged exposure to it would surely cause hearing loss.

Greg knew that the piece lasted for approximately 6 minutes, so he had to work fast. Grabbing at the crack at the back of the box, he tried to push on one side as he pulled on the other. At first, the material resisted; then in desperation, he really tugged and shoved, and finally the gap lengthened.

All the time, he was watching the bot, trying to make sure that it didn't notice his movements. Again, he pulled and strained, cracking the casing from top to bottom. This time, it made the shriek that Greg had feared, but it didn't matter. The noise just blended in with the music. Now, his only obstacle was to move without the bot noticing. Greg gave a kick to the bottom of his cage, and it seemed to move a bit. Pressing his shoulders backward, he gave a powerful shove. The top of his cage also gave a promising few inches.

He stopped and started thinking. *What if I do get out of here? How do I get out of the room? Is there a weapon that I can use? What weapons does the bot have?* Greg's adrenaline was really working for him as he prepared for the last move to escape from the prison box that had kept him for over a day.

He looked over at the bot which didn't have any obvious weapons other than the tools he had seen in its fingers. He couldn't dismiss the fact that its metal body could conceal more than one weapon. His greatest fear was that the bot might have a modified enforcer with an amputation modulation. This was a weapon devised by criminals for battle against enforcement agents and officers. The device could simply decode an agent's body shield, which was designed to withstand weapons fire. Afterward, it could damage any organ or limb that it hit, mostly by just shaving it off.

Greg looked to his left and saw a table made out of what appeared to be curtamite, a metal used for extrusion and replication. Once hardened, it would be nearly impossible to cut, even with a laser. Its reflective properties also allowed it to be polished to a fine sheen.

So, that would be the plan: get out of the box, grab the table top, and use it to defend himself and work his way out of the room. The only flaw in his brilliant plan was that he had no idea what was on either side of the two exits or how to get out of the structure that held the room that both he and the bot shared.

The music stopped abruptly, and the silence was deafening. A few minutes passed, and he observed the bot in a state of non-movement. It looked as if it was receiving a message. Greg waited anxiously. Suddenly the bot resumed playing the loud music until the piece was over.

Then it spoke, "Mr. Herrod, your time has come. I have been instructed to make your demise quick and painless."

Greg said, "I thought you said that after a few days, you'd let me go."

The bot just stared at him for a few moments. "Your agency has been notified that you are now deceased and that they will find your body at the new park of Zipher Knolls at sunshade."

Sunshade was a time when the second sun of Pertak had passed, and the third wasn't set to appear for a few hours. The reflection made the sky look as if it were shaded by a cloud or other celestial obstruction.

"We couldn't show up with a live body, now could we?" asked the bot who almost appeared to be smiling.

As the bot approached his cage, Greg knew that he had to act quickly. The bot was standing directly in front of him now. Greg braced himself against the back of the box, lifted his feet up against the transparency, and, in one motion, pushed as hard as he could for freedom. The bot, observing him, didn't register this behavior as a threat.

The wall collapsed behind him, landing Greg on his back on the floor. Shocked that it gave way so easily, he gathered his wits, jumped to his feet, and moved toward the table that he had planned to use. To his surprise, the bot hadn't moved or acknowledged the fact that he had escaped.

Changing direction, he ran directly toward the nearest exit. The motion sensor detected him and denied him exit, so he ripped a metal ledge off the wall and attempted to use it as a wedge for prying, but it didn't work. He bolted toward the other side of the room, running right past the bot and the cage that had held him into a windowless hall with a door near the end. Once again, he tried to exit but was denied. The bot spoke to him from the hall entrance. "Your escape attempt has been anticipated, Mr. Herrod. You won't succeed." A tool slid out of its forefinger and a laser beam struck him in the leg.

Greg grabbed hold of his thigh and let out a yelp. "That really hurt!" He rubbed his leg gingerly. *Lucky for me, he just grazed me. I've got to get up and out of the way before this pile of metal gets another shot off.*

***

While he continued to work on Liz's computer, Todd had sent Tim and Trina off to see if they could find Greg. He seemed to have disappeared into thin air. For some reason, GJED's computer couldn't locate Greg's gravicar. Tim and Trina headed downtown to the spot of Greg's last communication.

While Trina piloted, Tim sifted through copies of the files that Greg had requested from GJED's computer right before his disappearance. This would seem to be a good place to start looking.

As Tim thumbed through the files on his tablet, Trina reached over and placed her hand on his. Tim looked up; they both smiled, but neither said a word. Working together had brought them closer than just dating. The long hours and dangerous circumstances along with their ever increasing respect for one another's abilities had forged a loving bond.

Tim suddenly noticed that they were close to the first of the addresses that Greg had noted in his log. He pointed to a cluster of buildings and singled out an oddly shaped one that matched what Greg had described.

She landed her vehicle in a lot just shy of the building, and they exited. Trina remarked about how beautiful the evening sky was becoming. At sunshade, the suns were not visible, but the trailing light of one and the upcoming light of the other made for a spectacular view. They took a moment to soak in the beauty before continuing on their way.

Tim and Trina walked up to the strange building and had almost entered when Tim saw the marquee next to the door. Translated, it read "Specialty Doors."

Tim wondered out loud, "What does a door company have to do with Greg's investigation?"

Trina gave him a puzzled look, shrugged her shoulders, and said, "Let's find out. Greg's log said that he was looking for a Pertakian known as Wins Lafor."

They hopped aboard a transport pod and within seconds were standing in front of his office. They entered and approached the reception desk straight ahead. The bot at the counter inquired about the reason for their visit.

Tim simply said, "A colleague of ours may have been here yesterday. Could you please check to see if you have a record of his meeting with Mr. Lafor? His name is Greg Herrod."

The bot checked the available records and said, "I'll have to buzz Mr. Lafor." It tapped a pad on the console to its right which opened up a vidcomm. The bot introduced the pair to its boss, who agreed to meet with them.

Wins Lafor was a short and skinny Pertakian who spoke with a high-pitched voice. When asked about Greg, his face remained expressionless. Tim tried repeatedly to get a reaction from him without success. Wins was very calm and just replied, "I haven't seen or heard anything about or from a Greg Herrod. Now, if there isn't anything else, I need to get back to work."

As they were leaving, Trina looked over at Tim and asked, "Dead end?"

Tim answered, "It would seem so here. Let us continue with the next lead." They worked each lead in the order that Greg's log had given them but had absolutely no success. None of the contacts had seen or heard from Greg.

"This all seems a little suspicious, don't you think?" Trina asked.

Tim, nodding, said, "I agree. It seems that someone is hiding something, and Greg just happens to be in the middle of it."

Tim stopped and put his hand to his head as he thought. Trina was re-inspecting the leads to see if there was anything that they had overlooked. Scanning each page, she realized only one thing stood out. A number had been circled on the bottom of the third page. The circled number had a line drawn from it to the name Garnt.

"That's gotta mean something," Trina declared.

Tim looked over her shoulder and concurred. "This may be what we have been looking for."

"I wonder if...Hold on! I've got an idea."

Tim nodded approvingly, for he thought he knew where they were headed. When Trina landed in front of the building, he looked at her in surprise.

"I think you misunderstood the meaning of the location and the name," Tim said.

"Maybe. We'll see," Trina replied.

***

Todd was grinning in eager anticipation as he relayed back to the computer his answer to the second separthim code. Mike was enjoying watching him work. Todd was very pleased with the work he was accomplishing and wondered why he had ever taken a desk job instead of the field work that he liked so much.

One separthim after another began to give way as he answered the security codes, working with his comm uplinked to GJED's computer. Strangely, the work took his mind off Liz. As the separthims opened, he regained access to the different comm-based functions of Liz's apartment. The lights began working properly; the security system would arm and disarm; and even using the vidcomm for outgoing calls was possible.

The thing that bothered Todd was that he was unable to retrieve any data from the comm. He thought it must've been either damaged in the laser fire or deleted by the intruder(s). There were still a few more separthims to break, so he stayed somewhat optimistic. He opened another file, which offered another puzzle. Todd accepted the challenge.

With the lights finally on full illumination, Mike looked around the apartment for the first time. The disorder of the room was disturbing. He wondered what could possibly be so important that ceiling tiles and floor panels would be torn up. He combed through a pile of rubble. Nothing, he thought. It looks like the team has done its job. He sighed.

CHAPTER 7

Discovery and Desperation

Greg reached up and grabbed a panel off the wall, thinking that it might protect him for at least the next couple of shots. The bot quickly extinguished that hope. It reached up and turned a knob on its arm and quickly fired off a shot. The beam was very thin and the burst short. Greg looked down only to discover that the beam had gone through the panel and also through the wall beside him. It had gone so far that he could see into the room behind him.

He felt like a sitting duck knowing that he had absolutely no way to protect himself. He said to himself, *Think! Think!*

The bot spoke, "No more games. You have no defense."

"What do you expect me to do—stand still and let you kill me?"

"I don't see that you have any choice in the matter," said the robot emphatically. It raised its arm and let off another shot.

Greg, anticipating the shot, jumped to his feet and tumbled out of the path of the beam as it seared through the door. Looking back at the door, he had another idea. Since the bot was looking to kill him, surely it would fire at one of his critical body parts like the heart or head. As a spur-of-the-moment test, he stepped in front of the door. The bot fired upon him again, and he ducked out of the way.

Sweating profusely now, Greg picked himself up and leaned against the old sliding hydraulic door. Since he knew where the sensor would be, he placed his head there as a target. The bot stopped for a moment as if attempting to anticipate what he was doing. Greg thought that it could also have been recharging its firing mechanism.

The bot's countenance changed, and he could have sworn it was smiling creepily. It reached up and again twisted the knob on its arm. He hoped that it was increasing its power so that the beam would cut through the door. He stood still as the bot pointed the weapon at him and fired, not once but twice, in an alternating pattern. Not having anticipated this strategy from the bot, he did his best to tumble out of the way once again, but was hit full on his arm just above his hand.

The searing pain from the shot immobilized him momentarily, but then he heard the hiss of the door beside him. Freedom! Greg grabbed his arm and sprinted into the next room. The door hissed as it closed behind him.

Relentlessly, the bot walked to the door and gained access. As the door was sliding open and he was still dealing with the pain of his injured arm, Greg pulled at the panel which covered the door mechanism. He grabbed one of the two knobs inside and gave it a twist, knowing that it would reverse the door's motion. The door snapped shut with such force that it caught the bot's arm and severed it. The bot remained behind the closed door.

Greg snatched up the twisted limb and began testing the weapon to see if it needed to be attached to work. To his surprise, he found that the arm had backup power which allowed limited functionality. He fired a trial shot through the door at the disabled bot. Greg hoped that this would damage the bot further and prevent it from using any further weaponry that it may have had at its disposal.

Finally thinking that he could rest for a moment, he took a look around the large, triangular room. Choosing a corner, he grabbed a chair from a table and placed it pointing toward the center of the room. He figured that he would have an advantage if he could see both of the other corners.

He sat down to take a look at his arm when something caught his eye. He looked over to see a well-preserved police badge and a couple of other collectible items from ancient Earth set on a small, thin, marble table. All of the items that he picked up and examined had to do with law enforcement. Clearly, this marble table was also imported from Earth. Greg found this collection odd, given that this was the place of his captivity and attempted execution. He stuffed some of the items into his shirt pocket, hoping to examine them further if he actually made it out alive.

He grabbed the marble table and turned it over, noting the wooden legs. With his newly acquired weapon, he sharpened the legs to act as weapons should he need them. Greg found a cable which he used to hang the table around his neck with the legs facing away from him. He wasn't going to win any fashion awards, but it was functional.

With the weapon in his one good hand and the table around his neck, he made his way through the room, admiring the paintings on the two walls as he sought an exit. These paintings depicted 19th century Earth marshals from the Ancient West in the North American Sector. Too many things here led in the same direction.

Suddenly, a screen came down to meet his eyes. As it blinked to life, all that he could see was a dark figure which talked with an electronically altered raspy voice.

"Give up, Mr. Herrod. We didn't want to make this painful, but you're forcing that action upon us. We know that you've already sustained a wound. In mere moments, our bot will break into the room and kill you. If you give up now, we'll promise that your demise will be painless."

Greg gingerly touched his now raggedly bandaged arm. "Who are you and what do you want?" he demanded.

"That is all," replied the figure.

Greg insisted, "I want some answers before I die!"

The figure responded, "Ah, yes, I'll tell you about all of the crimes I've committed. I think they call that a criminal's prerogative. Once I've confessed to everything, you'll escape and tell the authorities. I don't think that's going to happen this time. You've been watching too many audivid programs. Goodbye, Mr. Herrod."

***

Tim and Trina walked to the door of the building and entered. An older style copper plated bot that was busily working there suddenly turned and asked, "May I help you?"

Trina replied, "Yes. We need to know if a Mr. Herrod kept his appointment here today."

The bot accessed its records with a blip, blip, blip, "Mr. Herrod did have an appointment with us today but apparently failed to show."

Trina looked at Tim and back to the bot and said, "Thank you very much for your help."

The bot returned to its duties as the pair headed for the door. Hissing, the door opened to let them out but stuck half-way closed.

Tim looked at the door and stated, "This place needs to be upgraded, and soon." He placed his hands on either side of the door and gave it a powerful shove. Just as he did, the lighting in the building turned off. Puzzled, Tim looked around to see if anything else was happening or if he had actually caused a power failure by shoving the door open.

Trina looked down the hall and saw that the walls were dimming and almost dark. "What happened?" she asked.

Tim tilted his head from right to left and said, "I guess I caused the outage by shoving the door open."

"The system must be ancient for that to occur." Trina posited, "Aren't you surprised that guard bot answered without asking for your credentials?"

Tim agreed, "Yes, that was strange. We need to go back and find that bot."

***

Greg was unsure about the warning that he had received, knowing that he had fired upon the bot in the next room and hadn't heard from it since. The room went dark, and the emergency power was activated. Greg checked the door before him, but it seemed to be stuck.

Moments later, he started hearing something banging on the door where he had amputated the bot's arm. Apparently, the emergency lighting had activated an emergency exit because as Greg squinted, he could see that a portion of the wall about ten feet away was open. He approached it, stooped over to enter the portion of the wall that was open, and entered directly into a lavish office. The door leading out of the office was also open, and Greg went through it into another hallway. He quickly found himself surrounded by four bots that looked very similar to the bot that had imprisoned and fired on him.

Greg, now showing his clear irritation, raised his newly acquired weapon and began firing wildly and shouting. He struck the bots several times each before they could even retaliate, making for a very loud and bright display. Given how far away he was from his prison, he figured that his shouts could now be heard.

Tim and Trina hadn't found the security bot but had made their way back to the entrance of the building. Tim heard the faint noise of someone shouting and also could make out what sounded like laser fire.

Without telling Trina what was happening, Tim started running toward the sound. The closer he got to the sound, the more he heard what was being shouted.

He heard, "Someone, anyone, help me! I'm a GJED agent."

Trina's ears weren't as keen as Tim's, for she hadn't heard anything but a muffled cry. She was asking, "Tim, where are you going?"

Tim didn't have time to explain but instead grabbed her by the arm and led her down the stairs.

"Where are we going?" Trina asked.

Tim just said, "Come with me."

As they approached, Trina could finally hear what Tim was hearing all along. He pulled the enforcer out of its pouch and set it to kill on contact.

"I've been hit!" came the cry from behind the door. Greg flung himself against the door and it flew open with Tim and Trina standing close to the doorway. Tim picked off one of the two remaining bots, and Trina took out the other.

"Whew, well that was interesting," said Trina.

"Thanks!" came the voice from the doorway straight ahead. An unshaven, hungry, bandaged Greg Herrod stood before them with a weapon in his hand and a marble table around his neck with four pointed table legs.

"I thought you'd never get here," said Greg.

"What is going on here?" inquired Trina.

"I think I may have a pretty good idea. Let's get going, I'll fill you in on the way back to Liz's apartment," Greg suggested.

On the way to Liz's apartment, Tim was busily attending to Greg's wounds and getting him up to his usual standards. Greg was doing his best to tell the information that he knew but his pain was overcoming him.

Both Tim and Trina knew that Greg was exhausted and needed to rest so Tim gave him something to help him sleep. "There will be plenty of time to solve this case once he has rested," Tim said quietly.

Behind her, Trina kept noticing a small, two passenger vehicle which seemed to be matching her movements. She maneuvered her craft to avoid being pursued. Just as she thought, the gravicar was definitely following her. She advised Tim to take a closer look at the two individuals inside. Tim grabbed a scanning tool and proceeded to hone in on the pursuing craft. He determined that the driver was Pertakian, and the other occupant was a bot that appeared to be wearing a uniform. He looked closer and realized that this bot was an enforcement bot...one of their own.

What is happening here? We're being followed by our own people. Tim thought incredulously. Tim looked over to the now sleeping Greg Herrod and whispered the question, "What have you gotten yourself into, Greg?"

Trina nervously ran her left hand through her black, kinky hair. Trying to get a grasp of what was going on, she asked, "What do we do now?"

Tim replied, "Use as much boost as you can on my mark. Steady, steady, steady, now!" Trina pushed the button on the throttle, and they jumped from their leisure pace to one that would certainly have surprised their trackers.

Tim was monitoring their progress and he looked at Trina with relief, "We had been targeted with class three particle laser cannons. I am relieved we were able to maneuver quickly." Trina, noting that no one was following, slowed her vehicle back to normal and continued her way back to Liz's apartment. Tim continued monitoring for any signs of the craft that had targeted them.

Just minutes away from their meeting place, Trina called Todd and told him they had retrieved Greg, and that he might have an idea of what was going on. The trio pulled under the overhang and parked their vehicle in the space next to Liz's gravicar.

Tim and Trina grabbed hold of Greg on either side and assisted him onto a levi-stretcher that Tim had ordered before they arrived. As they neared the door of the apartment, the wall slid open and there stood Mike waiting for them. Greg was still sedated, so Mike grabbed on to the levi-stretcher and pulled it behind him into the next room.

Finally, Todd appeared and ushered them all into the computer closet pulling Greg along with them. He started off by saying, "It's good to have you all back together again, because I think we can finally start putting things together here. As soon as Greg is ready and rested, I'll get together with him on some of the details that he may have. I do know, however, that this computer has been programmed by someone to keep us occupied. I've broken through each of the separthims in Liz's computer and even into the subroutines. I have complete control of the computer but no historical data exists. The only items in memory are simple commands for Liz's living conditions. I have an idea that as soon as a certain one of these separthims was broken, the data was uploaded to an off-site computer or deleted altogether.

Mike interrupted, "I need to go back to GJED."

"Another hunch Mike?" Todd asked. "The last one wasn't so great," he said with a smile.

"I have to check on something," he replied.

Todd demanded, "Mike, I'll need a report by third sunset."

"Right!" Mike replied.

Todd turned around, "Tim, I need your expertise to find out if Liz's computer transmitted anything during my shakedown. I also need to know who programmed the comm. Was it Liz or someone else? Anything you can give me, I want to know."

CHAPTER 8

Unseen Foe

As soon as he arrived, Mike hurried down the hallway at GJED and made his way to the elevation lift. After giving the command to his destination, he arrived seconds later on the floor where Yalan worked. He caught himself just as he approached her desk, slowed his walk, and wiped his brow.

Mike cleared his throat and spoke softly, "Yalan, Hi! How are you?"

Yalan looked up, jumped to her feet, and hugged him. "I'm fine, thank you. What are you doing here?"

"Oh, I just came by to ask you about something that you said the other night. We were discussing the girl who worked here before you, and you said that she'd left some things behind. Do you still have those things?" He tried not to look too anxious.

Yalan thought for a moment. "Well, let's see. I know I put them in a place where I wouldn't confuse them. Let me look in my desk." She opened her drawers one by one looking for the odd-colored memcards. She found nothing. "Wait! I put her things in a box. Yes, here they are." Yalan pulled out 6 memcards and gave them to Mike.

"Thank you! I think I know where to return these now. Hey! Would you like to do something later this week?"

She grinned and said, "I'd like that. Call me, and let me know what you have in mind. It's great to see you again."

Mike smiled widely and said, "OK, great! and thanks for your help."

***

Tim finished connecting his personal communications device to Liz's computer and immediately started issuing commands. The computer seemingly had been reset to defaults with only preferences being retained, so it was running quickly and receiving commands without delay. One thing was clearly evident; whoever did this wanted no trace of information found.

Todd gave the OK to allow a few of GJED's security employees to come take the computer back to the lab. Because they believed that data could be lost if moved, he had been reluctant to allow them to move it before now.

Trina was busy talking to Mike over the vidcomm, and it appeared that he was excited about something. Todd walked closer to Trina to hear. Mike told Trina about the memcards. He wanted to know if he should make his way over to the apartment.

Todd chimed in, "Mike, I appreciate your hard work on this. We've all had a very long day. Those memcards can wait until tomorrow. I suggest that we all go home and get some much needed rest and continue your investigation early tomorrow morning."

"All right, you've talked me into it," said Mike.

"No after-hours work tonight! Am I clear?" Todd demanded.

"Yes sir!" Mike said with a grin, then signed off.

Todd began clapping his hands to get the attention of everyone in the apartment. Everyone stopped what they were doing and stared at the Director. He spoke very plainly and with some insistence, "Everyone stop what you're doing and go home. We've made great strides on this case in just a few days, and I want you all rested so we can finish up. So, go home, get some rest, and be here early tomorrow morning. I have a feeling that we're on the verge of something big. Thank you for all that you're doing!"

One by one, they passed him on the way out the door. Greg was now off the levi-stretcher, feeling much better, and walking toward the door, when Todd reached over and grabbed Greg's shoulder and stopped him. "I know that you've gone through a lot over the past few days, and I want you to know, that I personally will make sure that you get your answers," he promised.

Greg looked Todd in his tri-colored eyes and said, "Finding Liz and what happened here is what I want most. I will do everything within my ability to solve this!"

"Thanks, Greg, I appreciate your resolve," exclaimed Todd.

Everyone had now left, leaving Todd alone. He scanned the room with remorse and whispered, "I will find you and put your kidnappers away for a very long time. I will! I promise you!" He picked up a picture of Liz, and gazed at it for a few moments. He gently put the picture back in its place on the shelf and spoke softly, "Lights off," and walked out of the room.

***

Mike was almost home, when he noticed someone standing outside of his sanda looking around. *Strange.* thought Mike. *Why do I recognize him?*

Parking his gravicar under the front of his sanda, Mike took the lift and entered from below. Now inside, he walked to the front door shuffling the memcards that he'd gotten from Yalan between his fingers and looked the individual over. He was a middle-aged Pertakian male with a burn scar on his face. As he watched, the visitor buzzed his comm.

Mike opened the door to the Pertakian and asked, "Can I help you?"

The Pertakian standing outside said, "Hi, my name is Fenoc. I wanted to talk to you about..." In the next moment, Fenoc grabbed his weapon and fired, hitting Mike on the arm that held the memcards. Yelling in pain, Mike dropped the memcards. Fenoc quickly shoved Mike onto his back, then grabbed the memcards and disappeared.

Mike surveyed the damage to his arm, got up, and started out the door after him. Fenoc was nowhere to be seen. Mike yelled back inside his sanda to his computer, "Perimeter scan, NOW!"

"Perimeter scan complete; nothing unusual is detected," replied the computer.

"Where did he go? He was just here! The memcards!" Adrenaline rushed through him. "What is going on here? This guy wasn't messing around. What did he say his name was? Fin..., Fan..., Fenoc!"

He headed into the office in his sanda, remoted in to his work computer, and ran a check on the name. The information that he was receiving was remarkable. In a weird twist, the guy seemed to have actually given him his real name. There was a picture of him, less the burn scar on his face.

Apparently, Fenoc had been involved in some illegal dealings involving espionage and even a charge of treason that had never been resolved. He had been in and out of enforcement camps, not because he had served his time, but because he kept escaping and being recaptured. The last camp in which he had been held was the most secure on this side of Pertak, but it too failed to keep him imprisoned for long. Among the list of traits alongside his name, two stuck out to Mike: bold and fearless. Mike suddenly became aware of the pain in his arm and touched it gently and said, "Bold, I guess! He never hesitated while attacking me." He read the last couple of lines on the report. "'Suspect is extremely dangerous; approach with extreme caution. Whereabouts unknown. Last reported to be hiding in or around greater Jubia.' Well, that part is certain, he is in Jubia."

Mike sprayed a solution on his arm which would act instantly to accelerate new skin tissue growth. He sat down and stared out the clear aluminite window. He loved looking out over the mountainous, rocky skyline during third sunset. It was so beautiful; he couldn't imagine living anywhere else. Mike was well travelled, had been to several planets, and even United Earth seemed dull in comparison to Pertak. He smiled. Director Sevick did say not to work tonight. I'll contact him in the morning. Now to settle in and get some rest.

***

Tim and Trina sounded the chime at Greg's sanda, then entered the unlocked door.

Greg looked up and proclaimed, "Hey, thanks for coming over. I wanted to thank you both for all that you did for me today. If it weren't for you being in the right place at the right time, I might not be here right now." His pride kicked in. "Well, I did have things pretty much under control."

Trina smiled and chimed in, "Well, in any case, you're safely back at home now. We're both glad to have you back. I know that Todd is relieved to have you back in one piece as well. I think that's why he had all of us go home for the evening early."

"Please tell us what has been happening for the past couple of days." Tim tucked his hand into his pocket and waited for him to answer.

Greg sighed, took a deep breath, and relayed his entire story to his two inquisitive co-workers. He felt like he could relax while being debriefed by friends in his own dwelling. They took turns asking questions while the conversation was being recorded by Greg's comm.

Tim assured Greg that Todd had already planned to send some agents down to the building where he had been held captive. Greg's chimes went off which startled all three of them. They all knew that Greg wasn't expecting anyone, and the door wasn't secured. Tim grabbed his enforcer and offered cover for his resting co-worker, while Trina went into the next room as backup.

Greg demanded of the computer, "Give me a perimeter visual and a positive identification of visitor."

Greg's new computer had a voice that was warm and confident: "The visitor is Director Sevick. Shall I allow him entrance?"

Trina poked her head in from the other room, and the three looked at each other questioningly.

"Um, yes, yes, let him in," said Greg.

Todd made his entrance with a smile.

The three of them just looked at him as if to say, "What?"

Todd looked at each of them in turn and said, "And just how are we all doing tonight?"

He was acting very strangely, they thought. One by one, they said, "Fine."

Greg asked, "To what do we owe this great pleasure, Director?"

"Oh," Todd said, "The pleasure is all mine. I just stopped by to say that you folks ought to be getting some rest tonight instead of working on this useless case."

Trina exclaimed, "Well, we were just talking to Greg...Useless?" she stopped, "Did you just call this case useless? But I thought..."

Tim was getting the sense that she should stop talking, and he stared her down.

"I guess so. Who needs a ride home?" Trina stood up and started toward the door. They all sensed what was happening and walked toward the door and exited. Once outside, they looked at each other and wondered if it was OK for them to talk once again.

Todd broke the silence, "Thanks for being observant, team. I was hoping you would get the idea. We just received an anonymous tip that while Greg was gone from his sanda, it was bugged. Our communications team was able to verify this using an ambient broadcast sweep. I hope you all didn't get too detailed in there. We also have reason to believe that Liz's apartment has been bugged. That's why I sent you all home early. This situation is far from being over as I see it. The fact is that we've scanned the apartment for any sort of radio waves or even subspace pulses that could carry such a transmission. Our agents weren't able to detect anything. If it weren't for a military intelligence agent from earth who happened to be stopping by and showing off some new gadgets, we would've missed it altogether. The channel being used is a newly-devised, top-secret, double-scrambled subspace channel wave made to look like an ultraviolet radiation disturbance. Now as I understand it, it can only be used during the peak times of Pertak's suns. Otherwise, the power signature would have alerted us. Unfortunately, having three suns does complicate things. Since we can't currently find the source of the transmission, we'll have to work around it." Todd took out his tablet and handed it to Tim. "Here are the times that we can meet and/or talk at these locations. Let me just tell you we're dealing with some major influence here. No one on Pertak has this level of sophistication."

"And for what?" Greg asked.

"I wish I knew," Todd responded.

Trina, Tim's ride home, started toward her gravicar when Todd said, "Tomorrow, I want you two to go back to the building where Greg was being held and turn it upside-down looking for information. I've already had the place closed down and put around-the-clock security on it until you arrive. I want to know who is behind this and why. Now go and get some rest, and I'll see you at the seventh hour."

"All right, Director, rest well." Trina said as they walked away.

Greg turned to Todd, who said, "Greg, you're with me." They climbed into Todd's gravicar and sped off to Mike's sanda.

Mike was just about to call the director, when his computer lit up and beeped. "Perimeter scan," Mike said.

"Scanning," said the voice. "Two visitors."

"Identify," continued Mike.

"One is Director Sevick, and the other is Greg Herrod," declared the voice. "Shall I allow entrance?"

"Yes, of course," answered Mike. The wall opened, and there stood the two of them.

Todd had stopped to pick up something lying outside the door. "Is this something that belongs to you, Mike?" asked Todd.

Mike looked at the object with some surprise. "Not exactly. That is one of the memcards that was stolen from me by a Pertakian named Fenoc." Mike snatched the card out of Todd's hand, brushed it off to see if there was any damage done to it, then took it over to his computer for further analysis.

"Mike!" said the Director sternly, "Come back, I need to ask you a question." Mike made his way back to the door with a distraught look on his face. "Does your perimeter scan reach to the end of your property on every side?" asked Todd.

Mike stopped walking and said, "What?"

Todd repeated the question only this time with a bit of joviality in his voice.

"Well, no," Mike said. "Apparently, there's a gap in coverage on one side. That's how Fenoc was able to..."

Todd stopped him by raising his hand. "Would you show it to me?" the director questioned.

"Sure," Mike answered, feeling confused. "It's right out here."

As soon as they were out of sensor range, Todd told him what was going on. Mike replied with an account of Fenoc's theft of the memcards.

Todd thought for a moment and said, "We're to meet at GJED tomorrow at the seventh hour. You'd better let me take that memcard. If someone has been listening in on our conversation, they are likely to be back. Maybe it'll shine light on some of this. Oh, and, Mike, be careful. The walls seem to have ears."

"I'll be there," smiled Mike. Todd and Greg made their departure as quickly as they had arrived, and Mike headed back into his sanda, where he seated himself in his favorite chair and tried to relax. Mike asked his computer to play some music, and just as he was drifting off to sleep, he jumped at the sound of a crash. He looked around and yelled, "Interior scan!"

"Nothing unusual detected," claimed the computer.

"What was that crash?!" insisted Mike.

The computer didn't respond.

"Computer, lights at 100% now!" Nothing happened. In the next instant, he saw the Pertakian who had shot and robbed him before standing right in front of this face.

"Where is it?" demanded Fenoc. An enforcer entered his field of vision, Mike's enforcer. "I can guarantee that it's not set to immobilize," warned Fenoc.

Mike was unsure of his next move. He reached into his pocket and to his surprise, he found the memcard. "OK, OK, Here it is."

Fenoc grabbed it from him and said to him nonchalantly, "I can't let you live; you know that." He raised Mike's enforcer, pointed it at him, and fired.

Mike awoke to his alarm and a new day. "A dream?" he wondered. He looked at his clock and hurried to get ready.

CHAPTER 9

Mangled Evidence

Trina, Tim, Greg, Mike, and the Director all assembled in the briefing room at GJED. The room was filled with paintings of very famous Pertakians and one human. Mike walked past and nodded respectfully to each of the Pertakians on the way to his seat. He was still wondering what he had experienced.

Todd addressed them, "I've had food catered in for all to enjoy, so please eat up. We'll start the meeting when you all have finished getting your food. I think I'll start with a Domarthian pastry."

They filled their plates and returned to their seats. Todd took a healthy bite of a red treat and began to speak as soon as he had swallowed it. "I've called you all here this morning because of some new information breaking on this case. We've learned, as you all know from our encounter last night, that whomever we're dealing with here has some incredible connections. We're dealing with some advanced technology and some very sophisticated criminals.

It would seem that this person or organization is able to hear everything that we're doing. Because of this, we've taken great measures to secure this room by generating a field around it that cannot be penetrated by any signal. This field has been pulsed-wrapped insuring no time elapses between power segments. Until we can be certain that we're not being monitored, any conversation that is sensitive in nature must take place within this room. Is this understood?"

All nodded.

"Good." the Director exclaimed. "Now, to get on with this project. Trina, you and Tim head back to the building where you found Greg. Go through this building and comb every inch of it. My understanding is that the building was populated solely by bots. Clearly, someone else was in charge of this operation. Disassemble as many bots as necessary to get some answers. Greg will show you the rooms using a diagram that I've asked him to create."

Agent Pilty opened the door to the room and yelled, "Director, something is happening to the secured building in the Blavs."

"What is it?" Todd asked impatiently. "Do we have any cameras down there?"

Jhan Pilty was half hanging in the door and cocked at such an angle, that he almost lost his grip and would've fallen to the floor. When he shook his head, he actually did. Struggling, he climbed back to his feet and gave the director a full answer, "Sir, I can tie you in. Give me one moment." A scene appeared on the wall which showed what seemed to be an imploding phase generator pulling the entire building in on itself. As the room full of agents watched in horror, the entire building disappeared. "Sir, there were four officers in that building."

Todd shook his head wearily and sighed. "Please leave us, Pilty." The group in the room could almost feel the fire coming from the now raging director. "This is it! I want everyone but Mike down there yesterday. Take readings with every piece of equipment you have. I want some answers!"

Without a word, everyone filed out of the room. "Now, Mike, let's have a look at that memcard." They left the conference room, sat down at a secure terminal, and began scanning the card for information. A question appeared on the screen which prevented them from proceeding further. It asked, "What do I mean to you?" Obviously, it was an authentication challenge, like the kind used on the separthims.

Mike looked at Todd and explained, "When I looked at this card briefly yesterday, it was encoded, and I didn't have time to attempt to decode it."

Todd opened a folder on his profile and executed a program that asked him to locate and identify the target information. He smiled and said to Mike, "Let's give this a try. It hasn't failed me yet!"

After a while Mike spoke. "Unfortunately, it doesn't appear to have circumvented the authentication protocols."

A thought hit Todd like a jolt of energium. His fingers flew over the pad, as he entered the words, "Nothing, absolutely nothing!"

Mike gave him a very strange look followed by an even stranger response, as the directory started to fill the screen. "My soul and spirit! But how did you...?"

The director just grinned as he went through the directories looking for some clue as to where Liz kept her personal files. He almost overlooked it, but he noticed the words, "noi siamo uno." The director immediately opened it. Looking over at Mike, whose eyes were very large with questions, he simply stated, "It's United Earth Italian for 'we are one.'" Mike just nodded. One section of that file said, "Message."

Todd spoke to the computer, "Computer, display the message on the wall to the East." Without hesitation, an image of Liz was placed on the wall. He could feel his heart slow to an almost unbelievable rate, but then it started pounding, as if it wanted to come out of his chest.

***

After hurrying through the corridor, the Pertakian male named Fenoc pressed his palm to the plate at eye level on the door. The wall opened to reveal an almost too clean room full of very advanced equipment and several Pertakians. He hated this room because it seemed so sterile that it made him feel uncomfortable.

In the corner of the room, a thin Pertakian female named Baluri was talking to two others. When she saw him enter, she approached him with a little box and placed it in front of his eye. "G-L-I-C-K," the little box sounded. "OK, Fenoc, you check out. Did you get what was asked of you?"

"I did, with no issues." Fenoc was perspiring so much now that it was visible. He wasn't used to being on the employee side of a job, but he had been persuaded with no uncertain terms to comply. Not only had he lost his partner, his lifelong friend from childhood, but now he had lost his dignity. He was working for someone he didn't really know but was compelled to obey. Sometimes he wished he had died with his partner or, even worse, been tried for his crimes and executed. Petty thievery was not his style, but it was all they were asking of him. Fenoc often thought he would probably be betrayed anyway, after this mission was over.

Baluri motioned to Fenoc to follow her to the table, where the other two Pertakian males were seated. "Absolutists," the thin female started, "this is our thief, Fenoc. He has been running some of our so-called errands for us and has done a great deal to help us in our endeavors. Unfortunately, we lost his partner in one of our first reconnaissance missions, but he has made good otherwise."

Fenoc looked the two Pertakians over. They looked like humans, but humans were colonists, and henceforth could not be a party to anything like this. He looked up at the male to the right of him who introduced himself.

"I'm Steith," said the male with the red mark that covered the entire left side of his face, and this is my apprentice, Dirzt. We're here to give you your next set of instructions, but first, I thought we'd all look in on Miss Paiste just to see if she might remember something more to help us in our task, maybe something to deal with in the future."

***

Todd heard his communication device chime, "Sevick here. This had better be good!" he said.

"Fraish here, sir, just wanted to update you on our progress."

The director took a deep breath, and continued softly, "Sorry, this is just a bad time....Uhh...go ahead, what did you find out?"

"Well, sir, the implosion succeeded. The entire building along with the parking lot nearby is gone. Since it left an incredible amount of debris for such an occurrence, I speculate that it was caused by a dirty antimatter converter set to overload. Such a device is only carried on spaceships that have light speed capabilities. Also, it must've been an older model at that based on the amount of debris it left. But of course, this is only speculation."

Half smiling, Todd replied, "Mr. Fraish, your speculations are better than some peoples' facts. Proceed with your assumptions, and contact me the moment anything comes up. Sevick out!"

Greg looked at Trina and Tim standing close together, as usual lately. He wondered what the pair were up to; obviously something had occurred while he was being held captive. Greg, with a big smile on his face, asked, "All right, you two, are you going to help me set up these antimatter displacement surveyors, or are you just going to stand there gawking at each other? Hmmmm?"

An embarrassed Tim reached down and tossed a matter stabilizer coil to Greg so hard that it almost knocked him over.

"OK! OK! I get the point!"

Trina giggled and gave Tim an approving look.

She picked up her tools and proceeded to where she would set up. After setting up the device, Tim and Greg went looking for debris big enough to analyze and determine if it were valuable as a clue.

One of the agents was examining a large boulder down the street from the place where Tim and Greg were standing. He gave a shout and waved for them to walk his way. Once there, they noticed something odd about the boulder. Aside from being large, it was also perfectly flat on one side.

Greg gave Tim a look of interest and a tinge of confusion. He pondered, "Why is everything near the implosion in rubble except for this piece? It appears to have been cut."

Tim tapped his comm and asked for a gravspanner and a heavy duty levi-lift. Using the spanner, they wedged the boulder onto the stretcher and pushed it over to the surveyors where they placed it as close to the center as they could. Using their device, they analyzed the boulder for any trace elements from the implosion. Just as they had expected, they found large amounts of antimatter within the boulder. They were able to determine by the shape, circumference, and density of the boulder what had cut it to its definitive shape.

Tim said with some confidence, "Judging by the size of this boulder, it was cut with a portable particle laser, the kind typically carried by a military vehicle. It is safe to assume that this boulder could have been a catalyst for the implosion. The sheared-off top could have been used as a deflection device, shielding the perpetrator from identification. Do we have monitored cameras in this area?"

One of the nearby agents said, "Checking on that sir. We should have something in the next few minutes."

A monitoring station was identified, and Trina made her way inside the building. A few minutes later, she was tied into the camera system looking through all of the available footage. Something caught her eye, so she stopped and played back the image. On the screen, she saw an unmarked military-style vehicle heading toward the center of town, but it was far from the building that had imploded just moments later. Unfortunately, it was impossible to know by the markings alone from which military it originated. DORWA was the only supplier of military vehicles, and it supplied all three land segment powers on the planet. The camera footage showed that once it had come to a stop, the wind started to blow violently. The footage went dark from there.

Trina was sitting next to a female Pertakian agent while reviewing the footage. "What does that look like to you?" Trina asked.

Agent Sehlia responded, "The wind made it appear that the vehicle was emitting some sort of electromagnetic pulse. We received a warning about a power outage just before the incident. This would seem to confirm our readings."

"That's very interesting," stated Trina. She tapped the comm on her arm and relayed the information to Tim and Greg.

"Understood," Greg responded. "Trina, see if you can get any further footage from the neighboring communities. I want to know where that vehicle came from."

***

Steith, Dirzt, Fenoc, and Baluri entered the room where Liz Paiste was being held. These Pertakians were extreme exclusionists who had dreams of a Pertak free of humans, Ciness, Domarthians, and any other outsider that might visit or live on their planet. They believed the world had been more peaceful before outsiders had colonized it and that these outside influences were causing more trouble than they were solving. Their need to sprawl made for larger cities and more world resources being used. The aim of these extremists was total removal of the off-world parasites at any cost.

Dirzt looked over at Liz who was lying on a hard metallic bed with a thin pad between her and the surface. Her long brunette hair had been cut short by her captors, and she was still wearing the same outfit in which she had been taken captive. She had been cared for by a Pertakian doctor, who had brought her back to full health some days earlier. She was restrained both hand and foot to her bed, and there was a guard posted at all times.

Steith looked at the restraints which held Liz and barked at her guard, "What now, do we act like humans? Remove those restraints so we can have a chat with our friend Liz here."

Liz, now incensed with her predicament, huffed loudly.

The guard removed her restraints and moved to cover the door to prevent her escape. Steith continued, "Now, Miss Paiste, please have a seat in one of our comfortable chairs. Liz reluctantly climbed off the bed and made her way to the table where the Pertakians were seated.

She knew what was about to happen here, or at least she had a good idea. Her father had warned her of some Pertakians who didn't like humans or any other outsiders. From a little girl, he had trained her how to react to a situation just like this. She looked disinterested and downright annoyed at the proposition of having to be interrogated. Liz had no aversion to any species and had a hard time understanding the seething hatred emanating from beings like this.

"Miss Paste," Dirzt started, "do you know why we rescued you from the med-camp that had imprisoned you?"

Liz looked perplexed. "You mean, do I know why you kidnapped me and my doctor?"

"A precautionary measure that ensured that you were cared for properly," he said. "Have we not nursed you back to health and allowed you to heal completely? We've given you shelter, nourishment, and security. I think you could be a little more grateful and accommodating."

Liz questioned, "What is it exactly that you want from me? I'm guessing that you have some reason for holding me here."

Steith seized the opportunity to speak, "We want you to tell us about yourself and your family. Who is your father, and what does he do? Also, why it is that you have so much security surrounding you."

Liz started off by telling how she had come to Pertak from United Earth as a little girl with her parents and added that she had recently started working at GJED.

Steith insisted, "Who is your father, and what does he do?

Liz looked confused, "My father? What does he have to do with this?" She knew better than to disclose that he was an ambassador and one of the original colonists from United Earth. Liz remembered what her father had told her his occupation was before his assignment on Pertak. She stated, "My father is a minister. He helps people find their way."

Fenoc snapped, "A minister of what, lies? I've been to your apartment. There's more security there than anything GJED has. My friend and partner died there. What's that about, huh?"

Unfazed, Liz said, "I'm sure I have no idea what you're referring to. I had my security system installed by a local security company who claimed that they would keep me safe. Perhaps, you could talk with them about it."

Fenoc's tri-blue eyes flared, and he shot back, "I'll do that, and when I find out that you're lying, I'll come back and..."

Steith blurted, "That's quite enough, Fenoc. Please return to your duties."

Fenoc murmured under his breath as he stormed out of the room.

Liz felt good about her performance so far. She thought that her father had taught her well and that he would be pleased. His caution to her was to act as if she knew nothing beyond her little world, as if she truly was just a secretary at GJED and nothing more. Well, she thought, it kinda is true. I don't really know anything that my father does. He doesn't tell me enough to get me into trouble. I just need to keep his identity safe.

"Miss Paste, how long have you been working at GJED?" asked Steith.

Liz answered, "I've been working as a secretary second-class for about three months now. Why? What information would I have that might be important to you?" She figured that if she offered information, they might not push too much further about her father.

"We'll soon see," replied Steith.

CHAPTER 10

Unexpected Revelation

Tim and Greg were finishing their measurements of the area where the building implosion had occurred. They estimated that only something like a spaceship would have had enough power to generate sufficient amounts of antimatter to cause an implosion of this magnitude. This seemed surreal to the two of them.

"Was it so important for us not to have what apparently was inside that complex, that they felt the need to utterly destroy it?" pondered Greg.

"Well, it is an effective means of making sure that nothing is ever discovered here," stated Tim. He tapped his comm and spoke, "Trina, have you found anything more about that vehicle?"

"The other sectors aren't being as helpful as this one. Two of them have told me *no* and the other one was so far out that it wouldn't make any difference. It could have come from anywhere," she responded.

Tim wrapped it up, "So, let me understand your theory on this. First, this military vehicle appeared, cut this boulder with a particle laser for reflection, and emitted an electromagnetic pulse to destroy any ability to see what was going to happen next. Second, a spaceship bounced the beam of an antimatter weapon off the sheared-off boulder and disintegrated the building?"

"Precisely," said Trina, happy that he had understood what she was saying. "I'm so glad that we're on the same page."

Tim responded, "I was merely restating what I believed you were surmising. I was not necessarily agreeing with you. I think we should take the evidence that we have back to GJED."

"See you there," said Trina.

Greg was going through the rubble, but he couldn't concentrate. All he could think about was that because of him, four officers had died. He ran his hand through his thick blonde hair. "I need to get out of here, Tim. I'm not doing well. I thought I could handle it, but clearly it's too soon for me to be back here."

Tim's attempt to comfort came at a strange angle. "You did not cause this, Greg; however, you may have been the catalyst for it. We all have our duties to perform, and these officers knew the risks involved."

Greg wasn't comforted. "Let's head back to GJED."

***

Mike's curiosity was getting the best of him. He was watching as Todd stared at the image of Liz on the wall, and it was clear that he was visibly shaken by it. Mike questioned, "What do you know about Liz? How did the two of you meet?"

Todd was still looking at the image and ignored Mike's question. He spoke to the computer, "Playback file from the beginning."

Liz's image didn't move, but she did speak. "My name is Liz Paiste. I have been compiling a list of items which have come to my attention over my time here at GJED." She then started listing names of people and processes which needed to be improved. This list included several people that worked on her floor. It seemed that she just needed to get this off her chest. Mike paced back and forth as she droned on and on about everything that was apparently a big deal to a secretary.

Mike excused himself to head back to his office. Todd waved. He was fascinated that she had made an effort to create such a record. This and the fact that someone went to great lengths to retrieve it made Todd even more intent on listening until she was completely finished.

Near the end of the recording, she said something that didn't make any sense. She said, "I have doubled up every two parax (a Pertakian measure of time with an approximation of a minute and a half) and I can't hear it, so I doubled up every two point one parax, and now it's fine." The recording ended soon after.

"Computer, go back to where she was talking about the parax." He listened closely, again and again. "That makes no sense," he said out loud. "Computer, double up the words *every two point one parax* and temporarily remove everything in between."

The computer took a moment. "Done," said the voice.

Todd was more curious than ever, "Computer, playback the edited message." The sound was garbled and monotone, but that was to be expected.

Her message was clear: "Upon hearing, contact father, William Taylor."

"William Taylor?" Todd whispered. "Liz's father is William Taylor?!" *He was one of the first human settlers on Pertak and a famous ambassador.* "What is going on here?"

Todd grabbed the memcard from the computer and walked to his office down the hall. He grabbed his computer and headed to the secure conference room where he knew that he wouldn't be disturbed or have his conversations snooped. Once inside, he asked his computer to contact the governor.

The governor's secretary answered the call. "Oh, hi, Todd. I'm sorry, but the governor can't be disturbed right now. He's in a meeting with some officials from the Blavs. It seems that they aren't too happy about what went on down there today."

"Tammy, tell the governor that I need to speak with him just as soon as he's finished. This is very important! Also, can you please see if you can locate William Taylor?"

"William Taylor?" Tammy asked. "Isn't he the famous ambassador?"

"Yes," continued Todd, "As I said, this is very important."

"I'll make sure the governor gets the message and see what I can do to track down William Taylor."

***

Trina met Tim and Greg at GJED, where they had their bots unload the heavy boulder and other debris from the implosion. They headed up to the secure conference room where Todd was still working. Once inside, he inquired, "What did you find down there?"

Trina relayed the entire story to the director along with her theory.

Todd looked over at Tim and Greg. "Are you buying this theory?"

Tim spoke first. "It does have its merits; however, we have no proof. It's impossible to know exactly what happened. We just know that anything that could have given us an indication of what happened to Greg has been destroyed."

"Well, not everything was destroyed," he said. "I do have a few mementos from my stay there." He reached inside his jacket, pulled out the items that he had transferred from his shirt pocket earlier, and laid them on the table.

Todd looked at Greg. "You're going to have to tell us the story behind these. Have you had any of them checked out?"

Shaking his head, Greg said, "Honestly, I forgot all about them until just now. They seem to be ancient Earth police adornments." He told the story about how he had just gotten away from the bot, stolen its weapon, and had a few minutes of privacy just before the lights went out. It was then that he had seen these items and stuffed them into his pocket.

"So, you stole them," Tim said with a half-smile. Greg looked back at him, unamused.

Director Sevick was trying to tie up some of the loose ends that the group had encountered. He asked Trina about the remaining evidence from Liz's apartment. Trina told him how the GJED computer had analyzed all of the remaining information within the core of Liz's computer and found that the computer had sent out some sort of signal just before its memory was wiped clean. There was still subspace residue on the device.

Unfortunately, the signal was irretrievable due to the total reset of the system. What they had found, however, by re-evaluating all of the data from the initial and subsequent imagizer scans, was that the scans didn't identify her assailant, just as they had feared.

"Wow, what a colossal waste of time," said Tim. "We have really gotten nowhere with this entire investigation."

Todd stopped him, "That's not entirely true. I have some new information on that front."

"Really?" questioned Trina, "What's the scoop, Director?"

"Well, I have a call into the governor that may clear up some of the mystery behind Liz's past and possibly tell us why she's missing. I don't know if this will help us find her, but I'm optimistic enough to say that she's probably safe. Once I have heard from the governor, I will call you all back to let you in on what's happening. Let's get moving on whatever is left of the evidence on the building implosion. I know the governor would like to have the Blavs' caretakers off his back right about now."

Tim wondered out loud, "Where is Mike anyway?"

Todd answered, "I think he got a little bored when I was going through some of Liz's personal files. He headed back to his office. Hey, are any of you getting together on your time off over the next two days?"

"Why? Did you have something in mind?" asked Greg.

"Well, I just happen to have the ability to get some tickets to see the Domarthian singers. I know someone who can get enough tickets for all of us if you want to go—Unless, of course, you're too tired of spending time with each other."

Tim and Trina looked at each other. "I want to go," they said in unison.

Greg was unsure. "I'll think about it," he said.

"No matter, let me know when you can," said Todd.

***

Jubia had an administrative building with offices for all of the top officials, including the governor. Mike was visiting a colleague there who was a security algorithms specialist. He noticed the governor heading into a meeting with some of the officials from the Blavs and a couple of people he didn't recognize.

Mike's colleague stepped out of his office for a few minutes and left Mike by himself. The office was next door to the governor's office, and he could hear some of what was being said. At first, he tried to keep himself from eavesdropping, but some things that he heard just couldn't be ignored.

"I don't know what you want me to do; I can't just have her killed."

"I'll make Greg disappear."

"Our dominance will begin with the destruction of Jubia."

"It has to look like an accident."

Mike was incensed. He wanted to storm into the meeting and confront the governor, but he knew better. His only option would be to take this information back to the director and let him deal with it.

Following an abbreviated visit with his colleague, Mike excused himself, his mind racing. His next thought was to try to get some more evidence to make his case to the director.

As he was walking to the lift where he had left his gravicar, Mike called an old detective buddy and asked if he could dig up some information on the governor. He stepped into his vehicle, closed the door, and asked, "Can you check to see if he had any ties to the organization known as 'The Absolutists?' Also, it would be helpful to have pictures of any known members."

Mike's case needed to be pretty rock-solid in order to accuse a high-ranking official of treason. "Make sure that you send this information to my personal account. I don't want to have anything like this getting into the wrong hands before I finish up," said Mike. He flew off and headed back to his sanda.

***

Todd's vidcomm notified him that the governor was contacting him, so he flipped up the screen. "Governor Blok, it's good to see you."

"Director," said the governor, acknowledging him.

Todd continued, "Governor, I wanted to let you know about a couple of things that I've discovered regarding the missing woman, Liz Paiste."

"I'm listening," said Blok.

"We were successful in breaking through the separthims in her home system. However, when we did, the communication device transmitted the data stored within to another computer. We couldn't identify the information or the whereabouts. We brought the core back to GJED and did some further analysis, but nothing else was retrievable. Also, I decoded some of her personal records and found that she had left a private message saying, 'Upon hearing, contact father, William Taylor.' Were you aware that she is the daughter of the ambassador?"

"Todd," said the governor. In all of the years that he'd been working for him, the governor had never called him by his name, only his title. He sat in rapt attention. "What I'm about to tell you is confidential. Are you in a secure area?" Todd nodded. He continued, "William Taylor is conducting a meeting with some extremely important and possibly dangerous people in the Jandia province. I understand that you've asked my secretary to locate him, but whatever you're looking to do must wait until these meetings are complete."

"Sir, are you saying that you have been aware of what's going on, and you haven't let me know?" asked Todd.

"I don't know anything more than what you've just told me, but I'm asking you to take the weekend off," said Blok. "Is there anything else that you can tell me about this building implosion?"

"Well, sir, we do know that a military vehicle was used to create a deflector for something large to set the implosion charge."

"That's hearsay," said Blok.

"These are the facts that we've gathered, sir," he answered respectfully.

The governor assured him, "When the time comes, I will notify William Taylor of this situation and have him contact you."

"Thank you, sir." Todd lowered his screen, disconnecting the call. *Well, he was in a strange mood. I've never known him to act this way. It must be the stress of having to deal with the Blavs caretakers and the sensitive nature of these talks,* he thought. Todd tapped his comm and sent a message to all of his team members. "By order of the governor, we're taking the weekend off. Anyone else want to meet Tim, Trina, and me at the Stabian Center to hear the Domarthian singers?"

Mike responded, "I'm going to be busy. I'll see you all back at GJED at the start of the week."

Greg said, "I'll be there. Get me a ticket."

Todd went home, changed his clothes, and headed out to the canyons. He wanted to clear his head, but all he could think about was the message that Liz had left using that memcard. It was clear that she had wanted someone to find it if anything happened to her. The governor had ordered him to stop his investigation, so that's what he would do. He decided to meditate to get his mind off things.

***

The next morning, Tim and Trina decided to spend the day hiking, so they headed off into the canyons with a picnic lunch. During Dile season, it was hard to know just when it would start to rain, so both of them wore shoes that would grip wet surfaces. Tim could see several people in front of them walking into the canyon area. It seemed to be sort of busy for a rainy day, but they decided to go ahead with their plans.

Since they had gotten a late start, they decided after only a couple of miles to stop for lunch. It started to sprinkle, so Trina decided to pull up her tightly curled, black hair into a makeshift bun. Tim watched her with wonder and smiled.

She spotted him looking at her and said, "You're not seeing me at my best, Tim. If I don't put up my hair, it'll frizz out, and you won't want to be seen with me at all."

Tim replied, "I am merely enjoying the view."

She commented, "The canyons are beautiful in this light, aren't they?"

Tim replied, "I was not referring to the canyons."

Trina just smiled back at him.

Finishing their lunch, they decided to take a detour into an area where they could see the wild desert flowers blooming. Tim picked one of the rose colored blooms and handed it to her. Trina graciously accepted and put it over her left ear.

Wanting to get a shot of the two of them in this moment, Tim pulled an imaging device out of his pocket. He clicked open the rear compartment of the device, pressed a few buttons, and placed it in the air and took his hand away. Tim spoke to the device to execute the commands that he had given it, and the device first climbed up into the air and recorded an aerial view, then behind them, and finally on each side. Once it had finished, the device displayed a hologram of the image that it had compiled. Trina approved, and they moved on to their next destination. Soon it was time to return home to get ready for the concert that evening. Both were looking forward to hearing and watching the Domarthians sing. Their voices were unparalleled in the galaxy.

***

Greg had been up very late working on a new prototype for a surface hardener. He wanted to make any material extremely durable simply by spraying a layer of the transparent substance onto it. Once he had been successful in a small sample test, he finally went to sleep.

The next day the sound of his vidcomm suddenly jolted him awake. No identification was announced, so he flipped up the screen to see who it was.

The dark-skinned Pertakian named Ptels on the other end didn't seem to know him but had some information for him. "Are you Greg Herrod?" asked the voice.

"I am. Who is this?" asked Greg.

"My name is Ptels. I live in the Blavs. I found a memcard in a broken strongbox near where that odd looking building was destroyed earlier. I ran it through my computer, and it had your name on it. If you want to pick it up, I'll be here," said the Pertakian.

Greg responded eagerly, "I would like to pick it up. Please send your coordinates so I can find you."

"Won't do you any good. Can't use coordinates in the Blavs. You should know that if you've been down here. Tracking systems don't work on account of the fungus," replied Ptels.

That's right, should've remembered that, thought Greg. "Where are you with regard to the destroyed building?" he questioned.

Ptels relayed the directions to him, and Greg assured him that he would be down immediately to pick it up.

Since his car had been destroyed in the implosion, Greg had to rely on either public transportation or someone to take him where he needed to go. So far, it hadn't been a problem, but this time it seemed to be very inconvenient. Greg's first call was to Todd, even though he knew that Todd wouldn't be happy with him following up on a lead during his break. Greg needed that memcard.

Todd's tone was just what he had expected. "Greg, the governor told me himself that we were to suspend all of our investigations into this matter."

Greg pressed, "I'm not investigating. I just need to pick up that memcard and get out of there."

Todd replied with some insistence, "The answer is *no*, Greg. I don't want to hear that you've gone behind my back regarding this either. I can't afford to lose any of my team. This has all of the markings of a setup. At the beginning of next week, you can take a couple of others and head down there, but not now. Am I clear?"

"Clear, sir," Greg said disappointedly. "I'll call that Pertakian back and let him know, and hopefully he can hold it for me."

Todd changed his tone and said cheerfully, "You'd better get ready for the concert tonight. I'll pick you up early."

"Will do," responded Greg. "I'll see you then." Greg went through his records to see if he could call the Pertakian named Ptels back. His vidcomm had recorded no number, and he had no way to respond to the call. Greg felt helpless and a little conflicted. He knew what Todd had said and understood that there must be some reason for the restriction but couldn't help thinking that he might be able to get some information from that memcard. He was thinking that this memcard could actually be the one that he had seen the bot handle when he was being held captive.

Against his better judgment, Greg decided to call Mike. Maybe the two of them could make the trip and retrieve the memcard before he was to be picked up by Todd to go to the concert. Mike listened as Greg told the story about the anonymous comm call and the Pertakian who told him about the memcard being found near the imploded building. He heard what Greg was saying but couldn't help thinking about what he had heard in the office next to the governor. The voice had said, "I'll make Greg disappear." Mike contemplated that thought, as Greg was attempting to persuade him to help retrieve the memcard.

Finally, Mike stopped him. "Greg!" he said. "I can't tell you why right now, but you can't go down there. I won't take you down there, and if you try to go by yourself, I'll rat you out to the director. Just calm down and stay put. We'll retrieve the card, just not today. When I have more time, maybe tomorrow, I can fill you in on the rest. Make sure you don't discuss this conversation with anyone."

Greg, now feeling totally dejected, said, "All right, all right, I'll stay here until Todd comes to pick me up. Thanks, Mike, and have a good night."

Todd arrived at Greg's sanda and parked on the bottom level beneath the entrance. Greg, now dressed in his best black suit with his thick, blonde hair slicked back, was ready for the concert. He hopped into Todd's gravicar and closed the door.

Todd was dressed informally with a collared shirt, slacks, and loafer shoes. Greg snickered under his breath at his shoes because they somehow just didn't fit the look. Todd's large tri-jointed feet made the shoes look too large.

Greg caught himself staring, so he decided to say something. "Nice shoes, Director!"

Todd shot him a look. "Thanks. I had them replicated after watching an ancient Earth TV program called 'My Three Sons.' I thought they looked vintage, so I had to have them."

"Nice," said Greg.

As the two of them flew off toward the Stabian Center, their conversation trailed off, and there was an awkward silence. Todd felt that he needed to say something about the conversation that they had had earlier. "Greg," he started, "I want you to know that...well, what I mean is..."

Greg stopped him. "You don't have to explain. I'm OK with it. I'm sure that Mike already let you know that I called him."

"Were you going to try to get him to take you down there?" questioned Todd.

"So, Mike didn't contact you?" he countered.

Seeing the traffic getting busier as they neared the concert hall, Todd decided that he'd better concentrate on what he was doing. "We can talk about this later," he said. "Let's just have a good time tonight."

"Agreed," said Greg.

He received a call and answered it. Tim and Trina were waiting for them next to the moving walk which took them from where Trina's vehicle was parked to where they would be seated for the concert. Greg let them know that they would be there shortly.

Soon they were all taking the moving walk to their seats. This process was extremely quick and easy. First Todd sat in one of the available seats, scanned his ticket, and his seat moved him to the proper location. Once his seat moved, another shifted in to take its place, and the process continued until all of the seats were filled. When the four of them were locked into location, they were able to look at the view.

Todd grinned, "Well, it doesn't hurt to know the solacemar of Domarthia, does it?" The rest agreed.

"It's beautiful up here!" Trina exclaimed.

"Just wait until we get to use our front of stage access passes. That will ensure that we see the singers close up," added Todd.

The Domarthians had some of the most ingenious and impressive art and music talent in the universe. The singers were known for putting on a performance that would provoke happiness, sadness, anger, laughter and sometimes a combination of these. Soon, the concert began, and the four of them become so enthralled that they tucked away the gravity of their work for a short time.

Near the middle of the performance, the four of them decided to take advantage of their front of stage passes, so they once again scanned their tickets and were presented with the option. One seat after the other moved into place right in front of the performers who took time to greet each one. The singers asked if they collectively had a favorite song which they would like the group to sing. Trina was the first to mention her favorite love ballad, and the rest agreed. The largest Domarthian male sang one of the parts of the song directly to Trina which made her flush with embarrassment, but she was loving the attention.

Once the song was over, they were bid farewell by the performers, and their seats returned to their original placement. By the time the performance was over, the audience had experienced something special. The release of emotion was good for all of them.

After the concert, they decided to go to the cafe in the caverns. Todd remembered Mike's enthusiastic account of his and Yalan's date and thought it would be a nice finish to the evening.

"The name is Sela; what'll it be?" asked the large Pertakian female. Her attitude said that she wasn't thrilled to be there. "The Earth water is good, but it's not cold," she added.

Tim looked at each of his co-workers in turn and with their consent said, "Well then, I guess we will all have Earth water."

A few moments later, Sela returned with their drinks. She saw the ID card that Greg was fidgeting with, paused for several moments, and walked away.

"Todd looked at Greg and asked, "I wonder what that was about? It was almost as if she was going to say something or ask a question but stopped herself."

"I don't know," said Greg. "Maybe I was just bugging her."

They soon started discussing the evening and forgot all about the strange encounter. When they decided to leave, Todd waved for the bot and pulled out his ID card. The bot scanned it for payment, and they exited the café.

CHAPTER 11

Absolutists

Mike was especially eager to meet with Todd. He had worked through the weekend finding information on the governor that he thought might help him put the pieces together. What he had secured in the way of evidence seemed to him an open and shut case and just the way this investigation ought to end. He was going to walk into Todd's office and present what he had found, and Todd would certainly see things his way. After all, he had gained the director's trust by working diligently and not causing any problems. He was a team player and everybody knew it. His personal pep talk continued for the entire trip to GJED. "I can do this. I can do this!" he said to himself. He knew that accusing a high-ranking officer, such as the governor, wasn't something that he could do without real reason, and he had a reason.

He tapped his comm and announced, "Garend to Director Sevick."

Todd answered, "Sevick here."

"Director, can I meet you this morning? I mean, right now?" Mike asked with urgency in his voice.

"Sure, Mike, I'm just getting into the office. Meet me in the secure room."

Mike walked with determination from the entrance of the building to the conference room. When he entered, Todd was standing near the back of the room.

Todd greeted him at the door with an outstretched hand. "Now Mike, what seems to be the problem?" Mike took a deep breath.

***

Trina had picked up Tim and Greg, and the three of them were making their way back down to the Blavs. Greg had gotten clearance from Todd to pick up the memcard from the Pertakian named Ptels who had contacted him. Greg was concerned that because he hadn't kept his appointment, he wouldn't be able to find Ptels. In turn, Trina and Tim tried to reassure him they would do everything they could to find the Pertakian and procure the memcard.

Greg thought back to his captivity. It had haunted his dreams, and he despised the thought of going back there. What drove him was his insatiable desire to find out what could have been on that memcard and why his name was attached to it. Why had he been singled out for capture and almost certain death?

Tim broke Greg's train of thought. "You do realize this could be some kind of trap. It is highly probable whoever was holding you may be attempting to finish what they started."

Greg pulled out his enforcer and adjusted its power and beam width. "I have considered it, but it's worth the risk if we can put some of these pieces together. We still need to find Liz."

"Agreed," stated Trina. "But you need to proceed with caution. We'll back you up, but we both want you alive when we return to GJED."

"Understood!" said Greg. "We'll do this by the book. Now set us down over there where my gravicar used to be."

"Starting scan of the area," stated Tim.

Trina added, "Make sure to compensate for the density of the algae."

Tim replied, "Already factored in. There are five Pertakians in the vicinity, one male, four females. I am currently honing in on the male; he is about 40 steps due east."

Greg was getting excited now. "Let's go find him!"

Tim replied, "Are your body shields fully charged?"

Greg and Trina nodded in the affirmative.

"Turn them on, and be careful out there," ordered Tim.

In turn, each of them twisted the knobs just under their comms and activated the field. The field actually emitted a slight hum due to the power being generated around their bodies. Since they were enforcement, their shields would protect them from most weapon fire. Unfortunately, nothing was impenetrable, which made any enforcement agent a little nervous. The bad guys were always looking for a way to take advantage of a vulnerable spot and penetrate the shields.

Tim, followed by Greg, climbed out of the gravicar on the right as Trina exited on the left, and they met behind the vehicle. Tim pulled out his scanner and pointed in the direction of the male Pertakian.

As they drew closer, a female voice yelled at them from behind one of the visible rubbish bins, "Stop, right where you are!"

They looked in the direction of the voice. "We're looking for a Pertakian named Ptels," Greg shouted back.

The female walked out to where they were and asked in an unwavering voice, "Are you Herrod?"

Greg nodded.

"We've been waiting for you. Come this way, all of you." As they turned to walk in the direction that she was leading them, Tim kept an eye on his scanner. It appeared that they were moving toward the three other females. The female leading them opened the door to some kind of warehouse and ushered them inside. Greg now had his hand on his enforcer, not knowing what to expect.

Inside the warehouse, they looked around and saw doors of every size and shape. A sign high on the wall in the back of the warehouse said "Specialty Doors." Tim and Trina looked at each other questioningly. The other female Pertakians seemed to be busily working in the various facets of the warehouse, and none seemed to be the least bit concerned about the visitors.

Their guide said to Greg, "Ptels told me about his conversation with you." She picked up the memcard from the table and tossed it to Greg. "Well, here you are then. Was there to be a form of payment?"

Greg answered, "We hadn't discussed it, but I'll be happy to give you a credit chip in exchange for it."

"Good enough, it'll have to do." she said. A credit chip was roughly equivalent to one-fourth of a day's wages. She inquired, "Do you know what happened down here a few days ago when the building disappeared? Did you ever find out? I mean, the four of us were scheduled to be working in that building, but your people were guarding it. I reckon they all died. Is that right?"

Trina responded, "It was a very sad incident. We don't know precisely what happened down here, although we do have some idea. Did you happen to see anything beforehand that seemed strange?"

Pointing at Greg, she said, "A few days before that, I saw him fly in, park his gravicar, and head inside the building. That's all I saw. Strange hair on that one."

Trina snickered under her breath and thanked the female Pertakian for her help. The three of them, still highly aware of their surroundings, walked toward the exit and headed for Trina's vehicle.

Greg looked at Trina and asked, "What was that crack about my hair?"

Trina just smiled and shrugged her shoulders.

***

Todd was listening with rapt attention while Mike laid out the case before him. He explained how he had been visiting a friend and had overheard the few phrases that made him a little suspicious. He had spent the last few days looking into how the governor might be involved with some radical organizations.

Todd was skeptical and warned Mike that without real solid evidence, he had better not attempt to accuse the governor of any wrongdoing. All of this, Mike already knew. He had been hoping something he was saying would spark an interest, and Todd would see things his way. "Mike, I understand that you thought you heard some rather treasonous things in the next room, but you and I both know, unless you heard what was being said in person and from whomever's mouth it came...I'm just saying that you probably heard it wrong. As a matter of fact, let me check in on Greg."

"Wait, where is Greg?" asked Mike.

"I spoke with the Governor this morning who gave me the go-ahead to allow Tim, Trina, and Greg to head back to the Blavs in order to retrieve the memcard that a certain Pertakian offered to hand over to Greg. Why?" asked Todd.

Mike's shouted, "You've got to get them out of there! They're walking into a trap!"

Todd tapped his comm and said, "Sevick to Herrod."

Greg answered, "Herrod here, sir."

"Greg, what's going on down there? Is everything all right?"

"Fine, sir, we've retrieved the memcard and are heading back to Trina's gravicar now."

As soon as the words left his mouth, Greg's enforcement shield was hit by a laser bolt. The three of them were out in the open next to the imploded building. His shield held, and he wasn't hurt, but another burst hit him, and this time the burst was much more powerful.

Tim had been watching his scanner when he saw the bolt of energy come toward Greg. He noticed that his scanner had picked up dozens of male Pertakians, but he couldn't tell where they came from. Trina thought she saw where the fire originated, so she pulled her enforcer from its pouch and fired in that general direction.

Greg scrambled for cover while the laser bolts rained down on him. It seemed odd that Greg was being targeted, but not Tim or Trina. They took cover anyway. Greg kept in contact with Todd as the firefight ensued. Todd asked Greg to send his coordinates, but Greg reminded him of the algae issues. Todd was thinking to himself, There's gotta be something I can do.

Just as quickly as it began, the attack ended. Tim's scanner revealed that the dozens of male Pertakians were no longer in the area. The laser bolts stopped raining down, and they checked to see if it was safe to leave theirs makeshift barricades.

After a few moments, Greg gave Trina the signal, and she, followed by Tim, walked quickly toward the vehicle without incident. Deciding all was clear, Greg picked himself up and made his way toward them, also without incident. They all climbed inside and took off toward GJED.

Todd turned to Mike with a look of incredulity and said, "OK, Mike, I'm listening. I'm sorry that I doubted you, but you have to understand the position you're putting me in. Tell me more about the connections that you were able to put together. I need to be able to do my own investigation into this matter. If there's something here, I need to have hard facts."

***

Liz, now lying back on the cold surface of her flat metal bed, was contemplating all of the things she had discussed with her captors. It had been a few days since they had interrogated her, and she felt like she had held her own. She hadn't divulged much, if any, information about who she was, who her parents were, or any sensitive information regarding her job.

She had played the part of a daddy's girl who really didn't know much more than what was just in her little world, and they seemed to buy it. The bed was getting a bit hard with just that flat cushion between the metal and her skin. She wanted to get up, walk around, and maybe sit in a chair, but she hadn't been allowed to do that unless she was being interrogated. She was bound by one ankle and one wrist which made it really difficult to sleep. Liz was getting tired of this situation.

Meanwhile, Liz's captors were discussing next steps. It was clear that she was a person of interest and perhaps a valuable one at that even though they hadn't gotten much from her yet.

The news that they were waiting to hear finally came in. Three GJED enforcement agents had been pinned down during a firefight in the Blavs. No one was hurt or killed, but this show of force had played into their hands. Their desire was to control things and make others fearful of them. Even though they hadn't officially come out and taken credit for the attack, it was clear that some organization was responsible for it as well as the implosion of an entire building and the imprisonment of one of the enforcement agents. This was just the beginning of their plan to take back what was rightfully theirs.

This was Pertak; no outsiders were welcome. Baluri would see to it that GJED understood the power that they wielded. Her next step was to contact the director and let him know who they were holding and what they wanted in exchange for her. They had collected enough data from the communications they had received through their subspace transmissions from both Liz's apartment and GJED proper to know what they were up against and were prepared for the fight.

Todd received a call from the governor's office right in the middle of his meeting with Mike. He answered, "Hello, Sevick here."

Tammy said, "Todd, the governor relayed the following information: The delegation to Jandia has completed its work. William Taylor said he will be in contact with you directly. That's all. Have a good day!"

"Thank you, Tammy. Give my regards to the governor."

Tim, Trina, and Greg walked into the secure room and took their respective seats. Todd asked them how they were doing and if they had been hurt in the incident down in the Blavs. They told the story of what had happened and reported that they were all OK.

Todd looked grimly at the recently seated trio. "I'm afraid that I've got some difficult news for you all. Mike has given me some information that, along with today's event, leads me to a conclusion that I would never have dreamed would occur. It appears..."

Todd's secretary cut him off. "Director, I have a Pertakian female named Baluri for you. She says that she has important information regarding Liz Paiste."

Todd thanked his secretary and told her to patch Baluri through. Within the next few seconds, a Pertakian female addressed him. "Director Todd Sevick, I will make this a brief conversation. We are holding the human girl named Liz Paiste."

Todd motioned for Tim to try to triangulate the call.

Baluri must've seen his gesture and said, "Don't bother trying to figure out where this call is coming from, Director; it will only send your trace to outer space. If you want to see the human girl alive and well, you will do exactly what we demand and when. We will be in touch within your next work day."

"Whom do you represent?" Todd asked. The video feed went blank. Todd huffed. "This day isn't getting any easier. Well, at least it seems that Liz is alive unless Baluri's lying. Tim, did you get anything on that call? Was she telling the truth about the call originating from space?"

Tim nodded and said, "It was precisely as she said. That is some impressive tech, unless they have got a ship out there."

Todd's eyes flashed. "Tim, you and Greg get some information for me on this Baluri person, and find out if there are any ships within the vicinity of the call. We need to know as much as we can about this situation before they make their demands. Go!"

"Trina, you were there when Tim talked with Liz's mother regarding her disappearance, right? You and Mike see if you can contact either her or her husband, the ambassador, and tell them that we're in a situation here that could use his diplomatic abilities."

Mike looked at Todd with shock. "Liz's father is William Taylor, the famous United Earth ambassador?"

Todd remembered, "Oh, that's right, you weren't here when I found out about her. It was on that personal memcard you and I were watching. There was a little trick to it, but you had already left. Anyway, now you're up to speed. You two get started."

Now that he had gotten them all out of his make-shift office, Todd decided he was going to continue going over the information Mike had presented to him. He needed to know if the governor was behind any of the things happening now. Something wasn't sitting right with Todd. He decided to go over the phrases that Mike had heard the governor say, one by one, to see if there was any correlation. He read aloud what he had written down as Mike had given it to him and started with the first one. "I don't know what you want me to do; I can't just have her killed." He picked up one of the old Earth police badges Greg had left there and stared at it. He wondered how the agent who had worn that badge would've dealt with the information before him.

Meanwhile, Mike and Trina had walked out of the secure room, down the hall, and into a large room with many terminals in it. Trina sat down and proceeded to retrieve any information that Liz's computer had regarding her parents. Since they had had no previous knowledge of her relation to the ambassador, they had failed to consider her parents' importance. Looking through the address book, Trina found an entry just listed as MD. Trina thought of two possibilities, but one had to be Mom and Dad.

An alert sounded on Mike's personal comm, and he excused himself to go speak to the party. He walked into a secluded area of the compound, made sure he wasn't being monitored, and began his conversation.

Trina called the contact listed as MD and received a recorded message asking the caller to contact the owner later. It gave no further instructions. She called the governor's office and asked if they had information on how to contact the ambassador.

Tammy seemed a little agitated that Trina was asking so quickly after she had called to let them know the ambassador would be in contact. "I'm sure that if you wait just a little while longer, the ambassador will contact you," she said.

Trina responded, trying to sound as nice as she could, "Director Sevick asked me to initiate contact as soon as possible. We have an emergency situation here."

Mike walked back into the room and heard the conversation in progress. He walked over and shut the vidcomm, ending the call. "Trina, you must not communicate with the governor's office right now. Todd will fill you in later, but you just need to trust me on this." Trina was a little upset by his actions, but she trusted Mike.

Tim was just finishing up his database search for a female Pertakian named Baluri. The lack of a surname made his search more difficult. Apparently, there were exactly 24 individuals with this name on Pertak.

He asked the computer, "Are any of the Pertakians with the name of Baluri associated with any crimes, arrests, or radical groups?"

The computer paused for a moment while working on the information, then answered, "Baluri Apendi has an arrest record for theft. Here is the list of items stolen and reclaimed..."

"Nevermind the list," said Tim. "Do you have a location for Baluri Apendi?"

"Whereabouts unknown," claimed the computer.

"That is it for me," Tim said with a sigh. "What do you have, Greg?"

"I just scanned the location that we received as coordinates while triangulating the call. There's literally nothing there but empty space. No subspace, ion, or nuclear trail exists either. She was right; tracing her call is impossible. You were right too; whoever these people are, they have some really impressive tech."

Todd was notified that Ambassador Taylor was on his way to the secure room, so he notified all of his team to return to welcome him. As they made their way back, Mike noticed how many people had gathered to watch as the Ambassador passed. He was indeed a celebrity, for he had made many deals with the Pertakians, for trade among other things. The two races had exchanged ideas, culture, and weapons. Now, it seemed, he was here to bargain for his own daughter's life.

Inside the sealed conference room, the ambassador greeted them all.

The ambassador was a formidable human whose dark but graying hair was long and thick, flowing back to cover his ears. He wasn't especially tall, but he had a presence unlike any other human on the planet. When he entered a room, no one could ignore him; he commanded everyone's attention. Todd was getting a sense of the reason for the secrecy in Liz's apartment.

The first words from the ambassador were a warning that that they should expect his visit to be met with resistance from the hardcore Pertakians. "The peace process is rarely met with trust. You must earn trust from every individual before peace can proceed," he began. "Please, update me on your investigation."

"Well, let's start at the beginning," said Todd. "I was going to have a date with Liz, whom we all found out later to be your daughter. I was called away on an emergency, which turned out to be a ruse. The next morning, Liz called me explaining that she had been hurt during a break-in the previous night. When we arrived at her apartment, we found her in desperate need of medical attention, so we sent her off with a couple of bots to MMC. Somehow, the bots had been commandeered, and they kidnapped Liz."

The ambassador interrupted, "My wife called a few days after this incident, I believe."

"Yes, yes, that's correct, and she talked to Tim," said Todd. "So, we attempted to get any records that we could from her computer but were unsuccessful. We were also unsuccessful at obtaining an atmospheric print. Can you shed some light on these failures for us? It seems that we've been stopped at every turn."

Ambassador Taylor looked thoughtful for a moment and spoke, "When Liz was first given this assignment, I wanted to make sure that she was safe. I had some of the best technology gurus from United Earth set up a security system which would protect Liz and keep anyone, including apparently GJED, from obtaining any information regarding her identity. I knew if anyone found out about the family connection that she'd be in real danger."

Todd stated, "We detected a subspace transmission which seemed to emanate from Liz's apartment when I broke through the security on the last separthim. The computer reset itself, and all we have been able to retrieve is a list of contacts, normal control commands, and macros."

The Ambassador answered, "Yes, I understand that the subspace communication was received by the security team who installed the system. The information dump resides securely within their data realm." The rest of the team was relieved to hear what had thwarted their best efforts.

Todd told the story about Liz's personal memcards and her cry for help hidden within the one that Mike had retrieved. Todd asked the ambassador, "Do you know anything about the building where Greg was held in the Blavs?"

Ambassador Taylor looked perplexed and asked, "Does this building have anything to do with my daughter?"

"Well, I suppose not," answered Todd. "I just thought that since you've been such a big help answering questions that perhaps..."

"Let's be clear, Director Sevick; I am here to find my daughter. I don't have any other interests at the moment. Now, if you would be so kind, please tell me the next steps that we must follow in order to plan for her safe retrieval."

"Understood," said Todd. "The Pertakian female said that she would be in contact within a day, so we need to plan a response. We already know that we can't trace the communication that she used. Tim, is there any way that we could turn our outgoing communication into a beacon of sorts?"

Tim already knew the answer. "Anything that is not a normal signal for communication is automatically filtered out. These systems were designed long ago with the necessity to eliminate anything that would cause interference. Also, if the filters were not in place, literally anything could be transmitted which could create a tremendous security risk."

"So much for that," declared Todd. "Ambassador, do you want to handle negotiations for your daughter?"

The ambassador thought for a moment and spoke, "I doubt that they even understand who they have at this point. I don't think it wise to let on that she is my daughter until we understand more about them and what their intentions are. Otherwise, they would have asked to negotiate with me directly. They did contact GJED after all. They are most likely just trying to feel you out and decide how important an asset they have."

"Of course, you're right." Todd excused himself and ushered Greg along with him on the way out of the room.

Once outside the door, Todd shook his head and said, "Greg, I feel like an idiot next to this guy. I don't know what it is; he's so intimidating that I just keep saying stupid things. Can you help me with this?"

Greg understood his dilemma and replied, "I'll do what I can to help. Maybe you should just ask him if there is anything else that he can tell us that might help. Then, when he's done talking, you can excuse him. That way, he's not there when you really need to be on your game. Besides, I don't think he means to be that way; it's just how he is.

Todd nodded and said, "I know. It's not every day that you get to meet a celebrity that you've admired all of your life."

The two of them strode back into the conference room and took their respective seats. Todd looked into the eyes of Ambassador Taylor and said, "Ambassador, you have my word that I will do whatever it takes to get your daughter back, safe and sound. Now, is there anything else you might tell us that could be of consequence?"

"I understand your position, Director Sevick; you have a large burden on your shoulders. I will await the outcome of your meeting, and afterward we can discuss this situation once again. Please record the next conversation with this Baluri, so that I may pick up any nuances in the communication. I have studied Pertakian speech inflections my entire career. I will leave you now. Do you have a place where I may meditate?" Ambassador Taylor folded his hands.

Todd answered, "Yes, sir, my secretary will show you to my office." The ambassador tipped his head and followed Todd's secretary out of the room.

Trina looked at Todd and queried, "Are you feeling all right, Director? I got the feeling that you were flustered."

"Quite all right now, thanks for your concern." answered Todd. "I was asking him questions, but I felt like I was the one being interrogated. I can see now why he has so much weight with our Pertakian leaders. I would imagine he could intimidate just about anyone into agreeing with him." Todd was thinking about his responsibility to make the governor aware of something as big as this situation. He wanted to follow protocol, but at this point, he didn't know whom he could trust, so he just put the problem out of his mind. He turned to his team and asked, "What did we find out about our current situation?"

All relayed the information that they had gathered. Essentially, they had found nothing new except for a possible last name for Liz's captor. The name they found was Baluri Apendi, and she had an arrest record. "Well, at least it's something. Maybe we can catch her off-guard by knowing something about her. Even if we don't know very much, she may wonder if we know more," exclaimed Todd. "Tim, I want every piece of equipment that you have tracking the next call that comes in from this Pertakian. If there is information in the signal, I want it found."

"Aye, sir," said Tim.

CHAPTER 12

The Ambassador's Daughter

A Pertakian clerk walked into a meeting room from his cubicle and apologized for interrupting. He had just received some interesting news about their captive and was anxious to report it. Baluri looked a little unsettled. She wasn't used to handling things like this. She had just recently been promoted after her predecessor didn't come back from a mission. The space phasing technology they had acquired had malfunctioned, and he was painfully disintegrated. What they were doing required them to take risks, and she knew that she was just another soldier in a battle. They were fighting for a just cause, and they weren't about to be dissuaded from that task even if it meant losing a few more soldiers in the line of duty.

"Yes, yes, what is it?" she inquired.

"Commander, I have just received the identification of the human we are holding," said the Pertakian.

"Well, go on!"

"It turns out that Liz Paiste is the daughter of William Taylor, the ambassador. Also, the ambassador is currently at GJED and has been in talks with the Director regarding this situation."

Baluri could hardly believe their good fortune. She smiled widely and said, "Thank you; that will be all." The Pertakian clerk left. Baluri turned to her counterparts and asked, "Can you believe the luck? We've got the ambassador's daughter. This will change things dramatically in our favor. We can literally ask for any resource that we want, and they will have to just hand it over. They would never dare risk losing someone of such value. Make sure that the ambassador's daughter is in good shape. We will want her to be presentable when we make the ransom demand."

"Yes, Commander," the two Pertakians said.

Baluri touched the pad on her comm. "Fenoc, I need you in here."

Within a few moments, Fenoc arrived looking a little ragged. He had been the only operative who was willing to use all of the technology they had acquired to get the job done quickly and efficiently. Unfortunately for him, some of the equipment was made very cheaply and had some bad side effects. He understood why he was doing the work; he just felt unappreciated and alone. Fenoc, trying to sound agreeable, asked, "What can I do for you, Commander?"

"Fenoc, I want you in charge of making sure that our communication goes as planned with the Director of GJED today. I want you to scramble, encrypt, and redirect the communication with no traceability as before. I don't care what it takes; they must not know our location. This could be the most important conversation of all, and it may very well tip the scales in our favor." Fenoc nodded and walked out of the room.

***

Back at GJED, Greg had finally found some time to spend alone in his office while awaiting the eventual call from Liz's captors. In his hand was the memcard which he had retrieved from the Pertakian female in the Blavs. He slipped it into the slot in his computer. The computer tried to read it but instead popped up a message that said, "One or more files are damaged. Shall I attempt to repair it?"

Greg was seriously getting tired of dead-ends. He shook his head and answered verbally, "Computer, take a sector by sector copy of this card, and attempt to repair it."

The computer worked for a few moments and popped up another error, "Sector copy failed. Try again?"

"Yes, continue!" said a frustrated Greg. Finally, the computer finished the sector copy and attempted repair of the file structure.

Once finished, the computer proclaimed, "Repair complete." A new window appeared on the screen with several icons. The one named "Herrod 2154777" looked like a video file, so he tried to open it. Before him on the screen appeared actual footage of him being held in the odd-shaped building in the Blavs. The camera views and the quality were poor, but it was footage that might help them piece together what had happened down there. He forwarded through the recording and noticed that it appeared to have captured several camera views as well. Greg felt anxiety while watching the footage but was excited that something had finally gone right. He decided to save a copy of this repaired file to GJED's main computer for later retrieval.

He opened the rest of the files in succession. One of them contained the names of some of the GJED agents while another contained several other names including two that he now recognized, Fenoc and Baluri. This could be very interesting, he said to himself. I wonder what other information is on this file. It appeared these files contained reports of incidents pertaining to visits to the odd-shaped building. He wondered why some names of agents appeared, and others did not. One thing that stuck out in his mind was that to his knowledge, Mike had not been to that building, so it made no sense that he would be listed in the file. Tim contacted Greg via vidcomm and informed him that a call was coming in from Baluri and that he should make his way to the secure room.

Greg secured the memcard and walked out of his office. He took the lift to the main floor and walked in just as the conversation was starting. Everyone in the room seemed to be tense, feeling the importance of the communication. Tim was busy making sure that every word was being recorded along with every nuance of inflection and movement. He was running multi-spectrum and frequency scans continually throughout the call.

The voice on the other end started, "Director, I understand that we have a very different situation from the one that we discussed earlier."

Todd looked sideways at the vidcomm and furrowed his brow. "How so?" he asked.

"Well, from what I understand, we are holding a guest of great value."

Todd responded coldly, "Miss Paiste is an employee, nothing more. Now let's get on with it, shall we?"

Baluri laughed. "Come now, Director, my understanding is that Liz Paiste is the daughter of the ambassador."

Todd tried hard to keep his composure but couldn't quite. "What makes you think that's the case? Did Liz tell you that? If she did, she probably thinks that it would earn favor with you. I certainly wouldn't put any stock in her claim given her present situation."

Baluri, now knowing that she clearly had the upper hand, said, "I have it on good authority that she is who I claim her to be. Her testimony is of no consequence. I am also aware that Ambassador Taylor is in your presence."

"What makes you think that?" asked Todd.

"Let's stop this dance, Director. I would like to speak with the ambassador."

Todd shot back, "The ambassador is indisposed at the moment. Once we have discussed terms regarding Liz Paiste, he may or may not be party to the negotiations. Oh, and by the way, our records indicate that your name is Baluri Apendi, and that you're a common thief. Why are you holding negotiations?"

Baluri was a little annoyed but undeterred. "The fact that you know my name and that I have a record within your system does not mean you know anything about me. As a matter of fact, I know exactly what's in..." Baluri stopped herself from going any further. "Let's get to it, shall we?" she continued.

Todd cut her off, "First, before we go any further, I need to see Liz to make sure that she's alive and well." Liz was ushered in front of the camera where Todd could see her. She looked well and didn't show any signs of abuse. "Liz, are you all right?" asked Todd.

Liz looked toward her captor as if getting approval to speak. She looked at Todd and said, "I'm doing as well as can be expected under the circumstances. They have cared for my wounds and met my other physical needs. It's as if I've been here for two point one parax; I have been distressed by the state in which I left my desk and my memcards."

One of the Pertakians grabbed her by the arm and yanked her away from the camera. Baluri reacted, "Enough of this. You tell the ambassador that I want ten million United Earth credits and his word that he will leave Pertak and never return. These are our demands, and they are non-negotiable. If he does not comply, we will not hesitate to kill his daughter. I will contact you tomorrow." The screen went blank as the call was disconnected.

Todd looked at Tim and asked, "Did you get all of that?"

Tim said, "I was scanning everything from the moment that the call started. I can analyze further, but I can assure you that they have taken multiple steps to cover their tracks. Not even background noise was allowed over the call."

Todd said, "The ambassador isn't going to like these demands. He has spent his entire career working with Pertakian leaders to bring about greater unity among the three continents and a lasting peace with United Earth."

"Trina, would you please retrieve the ambassador?" Trina nodded and headed out of the room. A few moments later, Ambassador Taylor entered the secure room alongside Trina. His demeanor was pensive but confident.

Todd spoke. "Well, Ambassador, they've made their demands. They want ten million United Earth credits, and they want you to leave Pertak for good."

"What of my daughter? Did you see Liz? Is she all right?"

Todd nodded. "She was seated before the camera, and I spoke with her. She said that they had attended to her wounds and her other physical needs. Then her conversation trailed off into talking about her office work, and they snatched her away from the camera."

Ambassador Taylor's ears perked up when he heard that she was talking about her workspace. "Director, can you play back the entire conversation so I may see my daughter? I can sometimes sense what she is thinking by her body language." Todd motioned for Tim to comply with his request.

Once the ambassador had completed his review of the conversation, he asked, "Can you show me her workspace?"

Todd replied, "Certainly, but before you start from scratch, let me tell you what I know about the situation." Todd told him Mike had retrieved the memcards from Yalan; then they were stolen from him. The one retrieved outside Mike's sanda had clued them in to the fact that Liz was his daughter. "So, you see, the first part is you. The second part is the information at her desk," exclaimed Todd.

"That's precisely why I asked to see her workspace," said the ambassador.

Todd again felt himself unable to think clearly. He just nodded and gestured the ambassador forward. Trina led the ambassador to the workspace where Yalan was seated and asked her if she would be willing to take a few minutes away from her desk.

Yalan smiled, looked at the ambassador, and said, "Ambassador, please let me know if there's anything you need, anything at all."

"Thank you, dear. I appreciate what you've already contributed to this process," replied the ambassador.

He seated himself at the desk and began looking through drawers, cubby holes, and any other cavities that might hide data storage devices. Once he was certain that there were no more data devices hidden, he asked to see her profile information and any memcards that might have belonged to her. Given access to her profile files, he combed through them knowing exactly what he was after but found nothing that looked familiar.

Todd pulled the discolored memcard from his pocket and handed it to the ambassador. It was clear that this was what he was after, and Todd felt like he was finally able to provide something for the ambassador that didn't make himself feel foolish. Ambassador Taylor put the memcard into the computer in front of him. He opened the directory of folders and noticed their compilation.

He asked, "You were able to break into this storage device?"

Todd said, "Yes. Just like the separthims at Liz's apartment, some of the security algorithms were from ancient Earth. Once I was able to successfully answer the security riddles, I was given access."

"I haven't been giving you enough credit. That is some impressive work, Director." The ambassador smiled for the first time since he had arrived.

He pulled a device from his coat that looked like a miniature vidcomm. He took the memcard, plugged it into the device, and a hologram appeared. "Show the image full-sized," he commanded. In a matter of seconds, there was a life-sized image of Liz. He spoke to her as if she were standing there with him, "Liz, can you tell me where you are?"

The hologram replied, "There is something blocking the transmission. It may be location-based or a distance issue."

The ambassador decided he would try to ascertain what his daughter had been doing before she was injured and then kidnapped. He asked several questions to which he received somewhat cryptic answers. He seemed to understand what she was saying because there were always follow-up questions.

Once the ambassador had finished, he put the memcard and the miniature device into his pocket. 'Director Sevick, I will need some assistance trying to locate my daughter before these demands come due. Can you provide an escort?"

"Absolutely!" replied Todd. Mike seemed anxious to help, and he offered to be the escort for the ambassador. Todd agreed but only if he would take another team member as backup. Trina agreed to accompany him.

The ambassador laid out his plans for trying to contact his daughter and attempting to retrieve her. He noted that in his daughter's hologram, she had mentioned the research she had been doing regarding some civil unrest in a small urban area of Jubia called the Blavs.

Trina looked at Mike, and they both shook their heads, "We've been spending more and more of our time down there lately," said Trina. She filled him in on all of the necessary details regarding Greg's capture and escape, the imploding building, and the retrieval of the memcard.

The ambassador finally understood why Todd had asked him about the building where Greg had been held. Everything was starting to make sense to him. "It's clear that this group has a reason for you to keep returning again and again. I think it's time to survey the area from a different perspective." Ambassador Taylor tapped the pad on his comm and asked for assistance.

The voice on the other end sounded like a male human.

"What can I do for you, Ambassador?" he asked.

"I need to have a thermal scan of the sector known as 'The Blavs.' I also need an overlay of the mapped grid on the scan and while you're at it, include any signal emissions," he said in a polite voice.

The human on the other end replied, "Sir, you do realize that the area in question is thick with algae."

"Understood," said the ambassador. "I don't care what it costs, get it done. I don't have much time to waste."

"Yes, Ambassador. I will see to it."

Mike asked, "How can you do that? Neither our tracking devices nor our satellites are trustworthy in that location. I would think you're going to get some skewed readings."

The ambassador simply said, "Position sometimes has its privileges."

***

Greg had asked for the director to come to his office to watch the video he had retrieved from the female Pertakian at "Specialty Doors." Todd sat down in the comfortable leather chair diagonally across from Greg. He made it a point to let Greg know that he understood how difficult watching this recording could be and that he appreciated Greg's bringing it to his attention.

The first part of the footage showed a split-screen of two cameras. Two bots were seen, one in the room where Greg would be held and the other in the triangle-shaped room into which he later escaped the first bot. At one point, the two bots moved out of both rooms and into another room where they disappeared for a bit. When they returned, they appeared to be carrying a levi-stretcher with Greg on it. Once inside the room, they rolled Greg from the stretcher into the box and activated its shield. During the next part, he was apparently asleep because the bots appeared to be docile. Greg fast-forwarded through this period in order to get to a point when some action was occurring. He narrated the activity for Todd as the hours passed within moments before their eyes. At one point, the second bot disappeared from view. Greg had been unaware that there were two bots in the room. The next part showed the bot open the ceiling, grab the memcard they were now watching, and insert it into a computer that appeared to be in control of the camera system.

The footage flickered as if it had gone out and flicked back on as clear as it had been. Greg started to feel a little strange as he was watching what played out next. The thought of his asking the bot to play loud music while he tried to escape almost made him laugh. They watched as he stepped into the next room after having taken the arm from the bot.

From that point on, everything went dark. Apparently, the camera system didn't have a power backup. At one point, Todd thought he saw something, so he asked Greg to go to 19.1173 in the footage. Greg obliged and let the footage run at normal speed. The figure that Todd saw had at one point during the loud music walked from the office into the triangular room. The figure picked up an item and walked away with it. *If nothing else*, Greg thought, *at least they will believe my story.*

"Well, I guess that's it," Greg said. "After that is when I fought off a bunch of bots and finally rescued Tim and Trina," he chuckled.

"I'm glad you made it out of there in one piece, Greg," Todd exclaimed.

"Me too. It just bugs me that the entire recording isn't here," complained Greg.

"Maybe it's everything that they wanted you to see," suggested Todd. "Remember, you did get this from someone you don't know or necessarily trust. It could be a ruse." Greg nodded.

Todd and Greg made their way back to the secure room where Todd had put the evidence against the governor together and started going over the pieces together. There were articles related to the governor's election, his family and their ties to a couple of unsavory groups as well as one mention of his being supported by the Absolutists for enacting a law regarding Pertakians' employment rights. This law essentially stated that a Pertakian would be given preference over an alien being. Another piece of information alluded to the governor's being a part of a conspiracy to have humans assassinated.

Todd looked over at Greg and said, "I see bits and pieces here, but I don't see the big picture if there is one. I do have a hard time dismissing the near massacre that you encountered down in the Blavs. It seemed to be orchestrated."

Greg added, "That was a really odd firefight. One moment, we were fighting for our lives; the next, we were walking out unharmed."

***

Ambassador Taylor received his much anticipated report. He wasn't telling much, but it did seem that he had a lot of resources. He asked if either Trina or Mike had actually visited the area. Trina stated that she had, so the ambassador asked her if any of the buildings looked familiar to her. She pointed out the now missing odd-shaped building and told the ambassador of the other buildings she and Tim had visited while looking for Greg.

Mike was amazed at the level of detail that the maps were able to provide. The maps provided information on thickness of algae, elevation of vegetation and buildings, water features, and were also capable of 3D scale and drill-down. Overlaid onto the map was a thermal layer which showed how much energy was being consumed in a single location as well as any signal emanation visible to their sensors. It appeared that a specific building was using a lot of energy and emitting a signal strong enough to disrupt communication.

"There!" the ambassador exclaimed. "That's the most likely place for them to be holding my daughter. Can I count on you both to be my compadres during this mission? My daughter's life may very well depend upon how well we work together."

"Yes, Ambassador," Trina exclaimed. Mike nodded. Because of her familiarity with the area, Trina volunteered to drive the others to the place the ambassador had chosen. Because this was a busy traffic time, Trina chose to stay closer to the ground where most gravicars didn't fly. Others wouldn't choose to do so because of the dust that a gravicar would create by flying that close to the ground. Trina had recently had a filter upgrade done for this very reason. It allowed her to get places faster without having to worry about damaging her vehicle. The avoidance systems would prevent the gravicar from flying too low, and she stayed within standard operating guidelines. The trip didn't take too long, but it was long enough for the ambassador to start his rendition of the ancient Earth religious hymn, "Amazing Grace." His voice was deep and resonant, and at one point Mike thought that the gravicar was actually vibrating from the man's singing. Both of them decided to just ignore him rather than say anything.

As they neared the compound, which consisted of a couple of buildings, the ambassador stopped his singing and asked Trina to hover not too close but within perceived communication distance. There appeared to be guards around the complex, but they didn't seem to notice them, at least not yet. The ambassador pulled out the small device from his pocket and inserted the memcard once again to activate the hologram of Liz. The hologram looked somewhat different now. It seemed to be more interactive. The ambassador asked again, "Liz, can you tell me where you are?"

***

Liz was shackled once again to the cold metal table where she spent most of her days unless she needed to eat or go to the bathroom. She had spent the day contemplating what she had said to Todd and wondering whether or not he had interpreted it correctly. She knew that her father was a very driven man, and that he would most likely find some way to retrieve her. She decided all she could do now was wait. She was really tired of being held like this. Her bones ached from being on the table for so long, and the Pertakians that kept her there didn't care. To her captors, she was an item of value to be traded, nothing more.

As she lay there, she felt a tingle on the back of her neck. Liz knew what this meant. When she was younger, her father had decided, since she would probably be in harm's way at some point, she would receive an implant, a homing beacon of sorts. This implant used a subspace signature, but it had limited range if its signal was actively being blocked. In such a case her father would have to get close. Once he was close enough, the hologram would tell him her coordinates as well as her vital signs. She now knew that her father was either close or was able to get a clear enough signal that her implant was responding. Liz smiled. She hoped her father would be careful in his attempt to retrieve her because she knew that these were some pretty desperate people, determined to do whatever it took to complete their mission and promote their cause.

The ambassador was gathering Liz's information from the hologram, thanks to their proximity to the building which held her. She seemed to be holding up well health-wise, but her position inside the building caused him some concern. From what he could tell, the signal was weak which meant that even a subspace transport would be nearly impossible. He needed to think of a means of rescue which wouldn't put his daughter in danger. It was clear that he needed a distraction of some kind, but what kind of distraction would draw everyone from a building? The ambassador was so deep in thought that he didn't even hear Trina question him.

Mike repeated Trina's question. "Ambassador, have you gotten any information from Liz?"

The ambassador shook himself from his thoughts and answered, "Liz isn't currently in distress, but she is in danger. I have a rough idea of where she is located within the building."

Mike said, "Ambassador, I think we should head back and plan this out or, at the very least, get some reinforcements."

The ambassador replied, "We don't have much time, but we must head to another location for supplies." He supplied Trina with the coordinates of the depot.

Trina didn't even question him; she simply complied with his request. On their way to the supply depot, Trina spotted a vehicle which looked very similar to the one that she had seen earlier while looking through the camera footage. It was apparent, to Trina anyway, that this was one of the military supply depots. As she flew around the last building before the depot, her vehicle was scanned for personnel, and they were cleared to land in one of the open spots. The three of them climbed out of Trina's gravicar and made their way to a very large and heavily armored door.

At the door, the ambassador put his hand against the pad. A voice greeted him, "Welcome Ambassador. May I know who your guests are?"

The ambassador introduced them as GJED agents. The door hissed as it opened and allowed entry. Once inside the depot, the ambassador excused himself, left Trina and Mike up front, and walked toward the back of the building and began talking with a man tending to the arrangement of some armaments.

Within a few moments, they watched him exchange some credits for hardware of some sort. One of the workers placed the items in a medium- sized box which could be carried by the ambassador. He said goodbye to the man, made his way back to the pair, and they left the building.

Following a reverse heading, Trina flew back once again to the spot where they had made contact with Liz's implant. Mike again asked the ambassador why they didn't just call for reinforcements and take Liz out by force.

"I don't want an all-out shooting match because Liz might become a casualty. Trust me on this, Mike. I've been doing this sort of thing for a very long time."

Against his better judgment, Mike agreed to the Ambassador's plan but took the opportunity to report in to headquarters. He tapped his comm and gave their approximate coordinates and their status. Part of the report mentioned that they were attempting to engage to some degree in order to retrieve the captive.

When Mike was finished, he turned to the ambassador and stated, "Ambassador, we are with you on this. What is your plan?"

Ambassador Taylor smiled. "Have either of you heard of Albert Einstein?"

Mike cocked his head sideways while Trina nodded.

The ambassador continued, "Einstein posited that gravity was a distortion of space-time. Gravity is how we keep our feet planted on the ground, and it's also part of how our gravicars function. With enough anti-gravity and considerable energy, the vehicles can fly and even float in place as we are doing now."

Mike was curious. "OK, so how does this help us?"

"Have you ever heard of an anti-gravity grenade? Basically, what it does is reverse the energy of gravity by emitting a burst of anti-matter. The effect would only last a matter of moments because antimatter is, by its very nature, unstable. So, I suggest that two of us go in to retrieve my daughter. One of us will remain here and send a few more grenades at the appropriate time for good measure," said the ambassador.

Trina felt a tingle go up her spine. "So, what you're saying is that we lob some anti-gravity grenades at them and hope they float?"

"It's a little more complex than that, but essentially yes," said Ambassador Taylor. He went over the plan with them, and when they were clear about their part in all of it, they both agreed to go forward. Mike volunteered to stay and replenish the grenades using the subspace transporter that the ambassador had just acquired. The grenades didn't need to be precisely placed because they were self-guiding. Once transported inside the building, the grenades would center themselves in each room and release their payload. They also understood that even while floating in mid-air, Liz's captors could fight. They were counting on the element of surprise and hoping that time would be on their side.

The other piece of equipment from the depot was a collapsible levi-stretcher with a thruster attached. This device would enable the Ambassador and Trina to float through the middle of the room. As long as they were holding onto the stretcher, they would be propelled through the building in a controlled fashion.

Everything was in place, and Mike was at the ready. All he needed was the go-ahead, and chaos would ensue. The ambassador gave the order, and Mike transported the first set of grenades into the building. The confusion inside the building was evident from the guards' reactions.

The ambassador grabbed Trina by the hand and said, "Shall we, my dear?" They activated their enforcement shields to guard against weapons fire. The ambassador activated his mobile transportation device, and in the next instant, the two of them were facing the guards. Using the element of surprise, Trina quickly dispatched both of the guards with her enforcer.

Ambassador Taylor swung open the front doors, and the pair began hearing the shouts of dismay from the Pertakians inside. Trina and the ambassador each pulled out a little box, pushed the button to open their collapsed levi-stretchers, and climbed aboard.

They worked their way through the corridors trying not to make eye contact with any of the floating Pertakians, but soon they started receiving weapons fire from one of them. He seemed to be angry that they had found a way to move about. His weapon was firing erratically simply because he had no way to brace himself for the shot.

In a matter of moments, they found themselves in what appeared to be a sterile room with many metal cabinets and shelves and very few people. Trina noticed a terminal she recognized from the vidcomm call when Liz's captors were bargaining for her.

She looked at the ambassador and said, "I think we're close."

He agreed and pulled out his hologram device to see if he could get an idea of where Liz was being held. He said to Trina, "This way!" They neared a locked door. Trina pulled her enforcer and blew a hole clean through the lock. When they entered the room, they found the gravity still intact and a very confused guard. Trina stunned the guard with her enforcer, and he sunk to the floor. There lying on her metal bed was

Liz, shackled hand and foot. She was understandably excited to see her father and reached out to embrace him. For a brief moment, he obliged, but quickly went to work trying to find a way to free Liz from her bonds.

Trina noticed outside the door that the floating Pertakians were not so high in the air and that some of them were finding ways to secure themselves. She hoped that Mike would send the next round of grenades quickly so that they would have a fighting chance to escape. She quickly secured the door.

Liz explained to her father that the guards used a code to unlock her shackles. The ambassador decided to take a more direct approach and used a lock-pick chip to brute force the code quickly.

Once Liz was free, the ambassador started scanning the area for jamming equipment. From the signal strength, it appeared that the subspace jamming equipment was housed in the next room where all of the metal cabinets were.

Trina realized that several Pertakians were right outside the door attempting to enter the room. Since the second set of grenades hadn't been delivered, Trina wondered what had become of Mike.

One of the Pertakians was shouting, "We know you're in there, Ambassador!" The ambassador gave Trina a puzzled look.

"Unless their sensors had my imprint, they should not know we're here. Don't make a sound; we all need to stand very close together over in that corner." The three of them were huddled together in the corner, when they began hearing weapons-fire at the door.

Within the next few moments, the Pertakians had made their way into the room where they found the unconscious guard, some unlocked shackles, and nothing else. "Search the complex!" yelled Baluri. "Don't stop looking until they've been found."

Fenoc strolled into the room and said, "Commander, in order to aid us in our search, we should turn off the subspace signal jammer. We could sweep-scan the entire complex within a few parax." Baluri felt uneasy about doing this, but she was also new to her position and feared retribution from her superiors if she didn't at least try everything she could to prevent their escape.

One of the clerks who had been scanning outside the building announced that the two guards had been taken out and that there was a craft hovering in close proximity to the complex.

Baluri asked if the vehicle was occupied to which he replied that there was one Pertakian inside. "Unless he's doing something suspicious, leave him alone, we can't treat our own people as suspects without cause," said Baluri.

The ambassador, Liz, and Trina were still standing in the corner, huddled closely in order to conserve as much energy as possible for escape. The ambassador's mobile transport device had essentially put a subspace transparency shield around the three of them. It was a poor-man's cloak, but it was effective for short amounts of time. Once he detected that the jammer was disabled, he transported all three of them back to Trina's gravicar.

Mike was stunned but relieved to see all three of them suddenly appear in the vehicle with him. Trina flew away as quickly as her gravicar would take them.

CHAPTER 13

Artifacts

As they sped away, Trina asked Mike what had happened to the second round of grenades that he was supposed to have delivered. Mike told her he had attempted to send the grenades to the same coordinates, but the frequency must have been re-modulated, and he wasn't able to penetrate their shields a second time. He added, "I think they found out what was happening and put a stop to it. I felt really helpless out here."

Trina said, "Well, from what we heard, if you hadn't been a Pertakian, they might have just pelted you out of the sky." Trina contacted GJED and gave them an update on their status. They acknowledged and let her know they would have a physician available for Liz when they arrived. The ambassador and his daughter held hands tightly. For most of the trip back to GJED, Liz remained quiet. Feeling ready for this chapter of her life to be over, she watched the landscape as they passed and thought back through what had occurred. Trina was certain that the Director would want to debrief her, so she spoke to Liz to prepare her for what was to come.

Once back at headquarters, Trina parked, and the four of them went inside. As they walked through the door, they were met by cheers and applause from the officers and agents. Liz just smiled while her father ushered her through the hall. The four made their way to the lift, up to the main floor, and headed toward the safe conference room. Before they went inside, the doctor examined Liz with a scanner to make sure she wasn't compromised with an explosive or communication device. Once the ambassador explained her implant, she was cleared, and they entered the conference room.

Todd hesitated only a moment before rushing over to hug her. The two embraced, but only briefly, for Liz was still unhappy about how this whole situation had started. She felt that Todd had allowed her to fall into the wrong hands and into a compromised state. Since she had been exposed as the ambassador's daughter, both she and her dad could be in danger. Her father's work was vitally important, and she didn't want to jeopardize it. She realized that she was physically, mentally, and emotionally exhausted.

Todd pulled himself together and went into director mode. He asked her, "Liz, are you up to discussing some of the things you've been through? I would understand if you feel you need to rest first."

Liz sat down in one of the conference room chairs and looked at Todd with determination. "I think we'd better get this done sooner rather than later. My captors have some pretty crazy technology, and I wouldn't be at all surprised if one of them showed up here. Let's get on with it, shall we?"

Todd said, "Very well then. We will be recording this conversation, and the archives will automatically encrypt the conversation and store it in our data atmosphere, which includes a number of places on Pertak and United Earth." Todd spoke to the computer, "Computer, begin recording. Debriefing Liz Paiste, daughter of Ambassador William Taylor. Miss Paiste, can you start back on the night of the incident and tell us what happened from your point of view?"

Liz started out by talking about the date that she had with Todd and how her car had malfunctioned making her late to the cafe. Once she had finally made it to the cafe, the greeter informed her that her date would not be coming but had left a message instead. So, she headed home, checked her vidcomm messages, and listened to one from her parents wishing her a happy birthday. She received another call from someone whose voice she sort of remembered but couldn't quite place. It was a male who wanted to meet her, but she wasn't going to have any of it, so she told him not to bother her. She was attempting to go to sleep when she heard a noise in the next room, but since she hadn't been notified of an intruder, she didn't think that it was anything to worry about. She put her housecoat on, grabbed her weapon, and headed into the next room to investigate, staying in the dark to avoid being seen. Almost immediately, she has shot in the chest with a laser beam and knocked unconscious.

The next morning, she found herself on her bed. Her enforcer was nowhere to be seen, and her computer wasn't working. Apparently, her vidcomm did work because Todd called her on it. She alerted Todd to the fact that she had been hit and fell back asleep. Agents from GJED arrived and had her put on a levi-stretcher and sent with two bots to a med-camp. On the way to the med-camp, the bots sedated her. When she awoke, she was in a med-camp room with a physician who was tending to her wounds. The laser shot had nicked her lung, and the physician had to repair the damage.

As she was recovering the next day, two Pertakians arrived in the room and demanded that both she and the doctor go with them. She heard one of them called "Tork." They were put into a med-camp vehicle and arrived at the complex that held her and the doctor for several days. Once she was healed, they dispatched the doctor because they couldn't risk their location being discovered.

Over the next several days, they kept her bound, hand and foot, to the flat metal table with only a very thin mat between her and the table. At one point her captors interrogated her for a few hours, and a day or two later, she was brought into another room to be shown on the vidcomm. She continued, "Then, my father and Trina came floating in on their powered levi-stretchers and shot the guard. My father picked the lock on my shackles, and we huddled in the corner while my father's transportation device hid us from my captors. Once they turned off the subspace signal jammer, my father transported us back to Trina's gravicar. After that, we headed here."

Todd looked understandingly toward her. "I can't imagine what you've been through. Thank you for your cooperation. We will go over your testimony and ask any follow-up questions when you're rested and ready to speak again."

Todd took the Ambassador aside and asked if he could retrieve the data from Liz's computer that was transmitted to United Earth once the last separthim was broken.

The Ambassador said he would contact the data storage facility and go through the logs to see if there was anything of consequence that he could share with GJED. He added that there were things that could be detrimental to the success of his diplomatic negotiations if he were to just hand over all of the records.

Todd thought about that for a moment. *Maybe that's why she had all of the security. It may not be totally about Liz after all. This certainly would shed new light on this situation.* The ambassador made his way out of the room to contact someone at one of the data storage facilities.

Trina and Mike were seated along with Greg at the conference table going over the past several hours and the information Trina had gathered during her brief entrance into the complex where Liz had been held. Trina told Todd they had gone to the military depot for supplies, then back to the place where they hovered and waited for the right moment to enter the building after the gravity was reversed using anti-gravity grenades.

Todd was inquisitive, "Whose idea was this?"

Trina answered, "It was the ambassador's idea. Once he knew approximately where Liz was, he had a plan to retrieve her."

Todd questioned further, "Did it not occur to either of you that this was extremely dangerous?"

Trina chuckled. "Well, yes, but he seems like the kind of guy who gets what he wants, and he's still alive, so I figured we'd just go with it."

Todd looked incredulous, "There is a thing called protocol, and next time I expect you to follow it. You could have gotten yourselves killed. If you don't want action against your record, I suggest that you take this into consideration next time. Just so you know, off the record, I'm proud of the work you all did today."

"Thank you, sir. I will do better next time. Thank you for understanding," Trina responded.

"Mike, you're awful quiet," Todd said.

Mike replied, "I didn't want to have any part of this. It seemed incredibly dangerous and could have gotten Liz killed. I only did what was expected of me."

Todd responded, "I can appreciate that, Mike. It seems that you were the level-headed one of the bunch."

Trina explained to Todd that the ambassador had made contact with Liz through the implant on the back of her neck and that was how they knew she was there and doing fine physically. She also told him about the transportation device he used to get them to the front door, transport the anti-gravity grenades inside the building, and transport the ambassador and her back to their vehicle.

For the next several minutes, Trina recalled in some detail the building they had visited. She mentioned how many Pertakians were there as well as the lack of humans. She went on telling about the height of the ceilings, how many halls and rooms there were, as well as what the communication room looked like. Finally she described entering the holding cell, hiding, and escaping.

Just as Trina was finishing her verbal debriefing, Todd's secretary called his vidcomm.

He answered, "Yes, what is it?"

"Director, the governor would like to speak with you," she said.

"Go ahead, put him through," said Todd. Todd motioned to them all to head out of the room. As the last of them left, Todd asked, "How are you, Governor Blok?"

The governor didn't seem anxious to chit-chat. "Director, I'll get right to the point. I've been hearing that one of your team members has been asking questions about my background and my ties to certain organizations. Today, I found out that some of your team, along with Ambassador Taylor, carried out an extremely dangerous mission to retrieve another member of your team. What kind of organization are you running over there? Are you aware of what's going on under your watch? Why wasn't I notified of this rescue mission and what precipitated it?"

Todd sighed and decided that he'd better tackle this head on, "Governor, I don't want to presume, but would you please answer a few questions for me?"

The Governor answered, "What kind of questions?"

Todd asked him about the situations and ties that Mike had brought up, being very careful not to identify Mike in the process.

The governor answered to Todd's satisfaction every correlation that Mike had discussed with him. He decided to delicately bring up what Mike had heard in the office next to his. Todd asked the governor if he could dispute the phrases that were said within the meeting between him and the Blavs administrators. He couldn't recall exactly what was said in that meeting but assured Todd that nothing inappropriate was mentioned. Just so there was no ambiguity, the governor did something that Todd had never expected. He offered to send over the recording of everything that was said in the meeting.

"Director, whatever it is that I've been accused of, I assure you that once you hear the recording, you'll be convinced otherwise. This was a standard meeting wherein we had to make some concessions in order to stave off a minor issue down there. Is this the reason that you've gone silent on me?"

Todd thought about his answer and replied, "Governor, do you mind allowing me to listen to the recording before I answer that question?"

"The recording is now available under your profile. Listen to item 715.699. Please contact me when you've had the opportunity to listen to it," said the governor.

"I will. Thank you, Governor Blok," said Todd.

Todd tapped his comm and said, "Sevick to Garend and Herrod. I'd like to have you both in here please."

Once inside the secure conference room, Todd asked them both to be seated, then spoke to his computer, "Playback item 715.699." The recording was clear and approximately 10 minutes long.

After it was finished, Todd looked over to Mike and said, "This was the recording of the meeting that took place when you overheard the governor in the next room. Did you hear anything that could have possibly sounded like what you've accused the governor of saying?" Mike looked confused. He started to speak, stopped, and shut his mouth.

Greg spoke, "Mike, I heard the phrases you mentioned to the director, but after listening to this, I didn't hear anything that sounded like killing Liz or making anyone disappear."

Mike finally spoke up, "I'm at a loss to explain it. I thought I understood what I heard. Maybe the walls muffled the sound to the point where I was hearing things incorrectly. I'm sorry for wasting your time, Director."

Todd took his time and decided to calm down before speaking again, "Mike, you've cost this agency a lot of time and resources, not to mention endangering my relationship with the governor. You've been a valued member of this team, and I'm glad you came to me about this. Next time, please come to me before researching things like this on your own. Your actions could have landed you in a prison camp doing hard labor for years." Mike just shook his head.

***

The following morning, Ambassador Taylor finished poring over the logs from Liz's apartment. Most of what he had seen was unremarkable. The logs were full of day-to-day things that Liz did. However, on the night that the intruder broke in and shot Liz, the computer noted some sort of anomaly with its programming which reset itself back to a few seconds before the anomaly. Each time it reached that point, it reset itself. This happened over and over again like an endless loop. The computer was programmed to know that after so many resets it required maintenance and eventually shut itself down. The bits and pieces of information gathered within the few seconds after the reset were incomplete and unreadable. That was the last information gathered until the GJED team was successful at resetting the system back to initial configurations. He relayed this information to Director Sevick.

***

Todd and Greg were meeting once again in the conference room to go over the information that he had gathered from the ambassador.

Greg said, "We still have no idea who did this to Liz. Is she up to speaking again?"

Todd answered, "She's on her way now. I don't know how much help she can be at this point. We've pretty much ascertained that she didn't see anyone. We need to know what the intruder was after and who attacked her. I think it safe to assume that it had to do with the group that held her."

Greg asked, "What about their location? Maybe you should have a team sent down there to investigate."

Todd shook his head, "I already sent Tim down there with a team of agents. That complex is now empty, not a Pertakian nor any equipment in sight."

***

Trina saw Tim heading into his office at headquarters, so she decided to see what he was doing. She walked in after him and sat down in one of his chairs without making a sound. Tim hadn't realized that she was even there. He was talking under his breath about something.

She couldn't be sure what he had said, so she asked, "What was that?"

Tim was caught off-guard but not startled. He turned to Trina and said, "I did not realize that you were present."

"I know," said Trina playfully. "That was the plan. You Cinessians are always known for your calm demeanor. I've never been able to rattle you no matter what I do. That must be why members of your race live so long. What was it that you were saying?" she asked.

"I was merely going over all of the facts in this case. I understand you were successful in retrieving Miss Paiste. Is she well?" Tim asked.

"I think after some rest, she'll come around," answered Trina. "I was given a pretty stern warning from the director regarding protocol."

Tim responded, "He is correct, Trina, you need to be more careful. We cannot afford to lose any more agents."

"Oh, and that's what I am, an agent?" she asked.

Tim half-smiled, "You know what I mean."

Trina replied, "I hope so by now." Their banter was interrupted by Director Sevick who was on his comm asking Trina to return to the secure room. Trina responded, "Tim is here too, Director. Shall I bring him along?"

"Tell Tim that he should come and give his official report regarding the empty complex."

"Empty complex?" Trina inquired of Tim. "Is he referring to the building where we found Liz?"

"I will explain when we get there," said Tim.

Trina responded to Todd, "We'll be right there."

Assembled in the secure conference room were Todd, Liz, Greg, Tim, Trina, and Ambassador Taylor. Mike was on his way but hadn't quite arrived.

Todd was asking Greg some questions about his capture while the others were listening. He pulled out the police artifacts and passed them around to everyone in the room. "These are items that were taken from the building where Greg was being held," he said. We don't know to whom they belong, but they could hold some significance."

The ambassador spoke up, "It would make sense that a collector of these items would know a great deal about their significance."

One important question was looming in the air, and Tim asked it. "Liz, what exactly was the intruder looking for in your apartment?" All sat expectantly awaiting her answer.

Liz looked at Tim and replied, "He never said, just that I had something he wanted. When I told him that I wouldn't meet him, I guess he decided not to wait."

"So, as far as you know, you were not holding anything of value in your possession?" Tim asked.

"I really don't know of anything that I have that would be valuable enough for someone to break in once, much less twice," she answered.

Todd said, "Let's be clear; we think that we've been dealing with Absolutists, so keep that in mind while we're discussing this matter. Ambassador, it would appear that the security system that you installed to keep your daughter safe acted as a red herring for us and kept us looking in that direction far too long. Obviously Liz has something to do with this or else she wouldn't have gotten the phone call and been subsequently kidnapped."

Ambassador Taylor spoke up. "I know that the Absolutists on Pertak depend on their technology in order to carry out their demonstrations of power. They probably didn't know who they had but thought that Liz, being a member of GJED, would command a hefty price for retrieval. Once they found out that she was my daughter, they figured they could kill two birds with one stone by getting a very large ransom as well as getting me to leave Pertak. I pose a pretty significant threat to their way of life."

CHAPTER 14

Mission Accomplished

Near the end of the ambassador's conversation, Mike entered the room and took a seat. Once the ambassador finished speaking, Todd turned his attention to Mike, who was now listening and trying to catch up. He knew that Mike hadn't been involved in the previous conversation regarding Greg's capture, so he picked up the police badge and slid it over the table to Mike. Todd said, "Hey Mike, what do you think of this?"

Mike picked up the badge and then saw that Tim and Trina were holding similar items. Without thinking, he looked back at Todd and asked, "What are you doing with my badges? Where did you get these?" As everyone in the room stared at him, Mike realized what had just happened.

He stood and bolted for the door, but Tim was already blocking his exit with his enforcer drawn.

"Mike, what is going on here? Am I to believe that you are the owner of these items?" Todd demanded. Mike stared straight ahead, stone-faced and wouldn't answer. He just stood there. "Mr. Fraish, take Mr. Garend to a holding cell. We'll have some further discussion regarding this matter shortly."

Tim placed Mike in restraints, took him to a holding cell, and checked him in. During the check-in process, everything except for clothing was removed from his person including his enforcer, enforcement shield, and communication device. Mike was placed inside the room, and the force field was activated.

Tim returned to the conversation in the conference room. With reserved excitement they spoke about Mike's involvement in everything.

Liz exclaimed, "Now I remember! I couldn't quite place it, but now I know it was definitely Mike's voice that I heard over my vidcomm that night."

Todd said, "Well, that's one piece to this puzzle."

Greg joined in, "There was an office next to the room where these items were found. Could that have been Mike's office too?"

Trina declared, "It makes sense now that I think about it. He never sent the second set of anti-gravity grenades in to help us escape."

The ambassador agreed, "Mike was very interested in my ability to obtain maps and other information about the area that we infiltrated."

Todd, now starting to feel the weight of betrayal, noted out loud, "All of the security that we have is for nothing if we have someone on the inside broadcasting all of our intelligence. No wonder they knew that Liz was the ambassador's daughter. It also makes sense that he wasn't really trying to break through the separthims. He was just wasting our time."

Trina said, "The very thought of this makes me ill. I am so angry at him!"

Director Sevick tried to calm them all down. "Let's not lose sight of the fact that now, at least, our questions are being answered. We may be able to coax some more information out of him before he faces the administrative council. The more information that we can gather, the better prepared we'll be for the obvious fight we have ahead with the Absolutists." Todd asked Tim and Trina if they wanted to have first crack at Mike to see if they could gather any more information.

Trina replied, "I'm going to have to cool off a bit before I can do that, Director."

Tim answered, "I will do it. Mike and I have worked together for some time now. I need to get some answers." Todd agreed, and Tim made his way to the cell which held Mike.

The cell was fairly stark with just a bed, a desk, and a chair. The walls were a grey color, and there was adequate lighting. Mike had made himself somewhat comfortable on the bed. Tim turned the force field off, let himself into Mike's cell, and told the guard to turn the force field back on.

He sat down on the chair next to the bed and began to talk. At first, Mike ignored Tim completely, but over time, he began to talk a bit. Tim asked him about the group with which he'd been working. Mike said that for some time now, he'd been convinced of the need for his allegiance to the Pertakian Absolutist cause.

He didn't seem hostile to Tim because he was Cinessian, not human. It was the human presence on Pertak that was the greatest threat to the Pertakian way of life. Tim asked Mike if he was the one who had called Liz the night of the break-in. Mike confirmed that he had indeed called Liz to see if they could meet. He explained that he was attempting to remove her from the situation and to keep her from harm. He knew that the break-in was going to occur that night, but he was powerless to keep her safe without blowing his cover.

"What did they break in to find?" questioned Tim.

Mike replied, "I wasn't really in on the detail work. I overheard the ones in charge talking about the founding document. That's all I can tell you."

"That is all you can tell me, or that is all you know?" queried Tim.

"Can we talk later?" Mike asked.

Tim nodded and said, "Sure Mike, we will speak again soon."

Mike grabbed Tim's arm as he was leaving and warned him, "Tim, be careful. These people are dangerous. They are willing to do anything to achieve their goals." Tim nodded and asked the guard to lower the force field. He stepped away and left Mike in his cell.

As he was heading back to the conference room, Yalan stopped Tim and asked him what had happened. She had seen him walking Mike to the holding facility. "What is going on? Did Mike do something wrong?" asked Yalan.

Tim bowed his head slightly and looked at her. "Mike is apparently guilty of espionage and perhaps even treason. At this point, we are holding him for questioning."

Yalan frowned and sighed. "I'm really confused. He seemed to really want to crack this case."

"Yes, he seemed to be a helpful operative. Unfortunately, at this point, it appears that his help was directed to a cause different from our own." stated Tim.

"Can you let me talk with him before you move him away from GJED?" asked Yalan.

"I will see what can be done." answered Tim. "Now if you will excuse me, I need to return to the conference room."

Inside the conference room, Todd and the Ambassador were speaking with the governor. Todd was briefing the governor on the events of the day. Tim arrived at precisely the moment they were to start the discussion of what information might come from a confession.

Tim spoke loudly so everyone involved could hear. "You will be relieved to know, Ambassador Taylor, that Mike was attempting to keep Liz from being harmed by luring her away from her apartment on the night she was attacked."

Governor Blok shot back, "Tim, did you find out what they were after?"

Tim answered, "The only thing that Mike mentioned was something called the founding document. He overheard a conversation regarding this."

"Of course!" exclaimed Ambassador Taylor.

"You have something?" asked Todd.

Ambassador Taylor explained that he had, in his possession, one of only two copies of the original Pertakian Constitution. One copy had been lost in a skirmish between land-segment powers, and the other copy was in the hands of a United Earth collector. He explained further, "To the Absolutists, this document is priceless. Even though the original Constitution hasn't been used in over a millennium, they still hold to what the original document proclaims. That is, Pertak must remain inhabited only by Pertakians. To allow other worlds to populate Pertak would dilute their society.

The Constitution that is now followed was drafted some three hundred years after the original. The Absolutists believe that if they can obtain the original document, they will have more leverage to force the governments to comply with it."

Governor Blok asked, "Why did you have the document, Ambassador?"

"Well, that's an interesting story. You see, when the collector heard that the other copy had gone missing, she decided to donate the only remaining version of it back to the Pertakian society. She is somewhat of a philanthropist and wants to see cultures preserved.

I was given the opportunity to present the document to the archives at the eighth centennial ceremony. My wife and I had it with us when we stayed at Liz's apartment just two nights prior to the incident. I'm assuming that the Absolutists picked up on the document's whereabouts using the security tag embedded in it," said the Ambassador.

The governor asked, "Where is the document now?"

"I presented it to the archives in Telor for safe-keeping, just as I had planned. It's safe and sound under some of the best protection known on any world."

Todd commented, "That makes a lot of sense. I think that ties things up a bit more."

"Director, keep me informed of any further discoveries." insisted the governor.

"Will do," confirmed Todd.

Todd's secretary called his vidcomm and he answered, "Yes, what is it?"

"Director Sevick, that Pertakian female named Baluri is on the line once again for you." Todd gestured at Tim to record the conversation.

"Director Sevick," Baluri said sternly. "You have one of my agents, and I want him back. If you do not wish to incur the wrath of..."

Todd interrupted, "I believe that you have that backwards, Baluri. Mike is being held because he broke our laws and will be interrogated and prosecuted. I understand that you've had to move recently. I hope your new accommodations are more to your liking." Todd smiled.

Baluri was not amused. "This will be your final warning. Let my agent go or suffer the consequences."

"You know I can't do that. He will be tried for his crimes after he is interrogated to find out everything we can about your terrorist organization."

"We are not terrorists! We just want to restore Pertak to its place of prominence. We have become diluted with Humans, Domarthians, and Cinessians. The founding document clearly states that this is a violation. Director, you are Pertakian. Do you not feel any sense of obligation to our founders?" Not letting him get a word in, she continued, "Of course not, you consort with the enemy like those in your presence now." Baluri sighed heavily and disconnected the call.

Ambassador Taylor cautioned Director Sevick, "I think it might be prudent to shore up the security on your facility and your agents at least until your interrogation is complete. This Pertakian female seems very intent on her demands."

Todd agreed and made a general announcement for all of the agents in the facility. He advised them to take extreme caution and to activate their body shields even while indoors. He contacted perimeter security and put them on high alert, which included increasing the strength of their perimeter shield. They would know if Baluri's associates attempted to transport into the facility because they would have a record of any unauthorized attempts. Todd was hoping that if they did attempt to transport in, his team could get a fix on their location.

Todd contacted the governor once again and reported the call he had just received and the actions that he had taken. The governor thanked him for keeping him up-to-date.

After the call was finished, Todd excused himself and said he was going to attempt to talk with Mike.

As he was headed out the door, Tim said to him, "Director, when I left Mike, he said he wanted to be alone for a while."

Todd turned on his rather large heels and said, "Well, that was a little while ago. I'm going to try to talk with him, Pertakian to Pertakian."

"I wish you success in your attempt," said Tim.

"I just have a feeling that he'll talk to me," said Todd as he continued out the door.

Mike was feeling restless in his cell and was getting visibly agitated.

The guard saw the director coming his way and warned him, "Sir, he's acting somewhat aggressive."

"It's all right. I'll talk with him from outside the force field. You may return to your duties," said Todd.

The young Pertakian guard tipped his head slightly, turned around, and went back to his desk.

Mike looked like he wasn't at all happy to see Todd. He spoke first anyway. "Director, why do you put up with the outsiders working side-by-side with us?"

Todd didn't answer his question but posed one of his own. "Why would you throw away your entire career to follow after a bunch of thugs, Mike? I've known you for several years; we've worked through many cases together. I never dreamed you would deceive us like this. What's worse, you could have gotten the ambassador and his daughter killed, and it would've appeared you planned to do it. Do you know how badly this is going to go for you?"

Mike looked at Todd with utter disgust and snapped, "This is exactly what I'm talking about. You're sticking up for them!"

Todd answered softly, "Mike, I'm not picking sides on this issue. I am trying to make you see that your actions were wrong. Can't you see that?"

Mike appeared to soften just a little. "Surely you didn't come down here to talk about ideologies. Is there something specific you wanted to ask me?"

Todd replied, "Yes, there is. Can you tell me who we're dealing with here? If you cooperate, I promise I will personally put in a good word for you with the council."

"It won't matter anyway. I probably won't make it to the hearing. They'll either come and take me or kill me," said Mike.

"I won't let them do that," promised Todd.

"You can't stop them!" insisted Mike. "They've acquired most of their technology by kidnapping and demanding ransom. They have stuff that most governments don't even know exists. Most of their agents don't even want to use the stuff, but there is this one guy who is willing to try anything if it will give him an advantage."

Todd queried, "Can you give me a name?"

Mike sighed, "The guy's name is Fenoc. I'm probably going to regret telling you that."

Todd looked confused and asked, "Isn't that the guy that came to your sanda and robbed you? I thought you two were on the same team."

Mike answered, "This guy does everything as if it's for real. If there's a chance it's being recorded, he'll even kill another agent just for effect. I can't tell you how much I admire and hate that guy all at the same time."

"Can you tell me why these people kidnapped Greg, tried to kill him, and imploded the building down in the Blavs?" asked Todd.

Mike shook his head, "I screwed up, and they needed to erase the evidence. Let's leave it at that."

Todd's comm alerted him to an incoming call. He stepped away from Mike's earshot and answered. Governor Blok told Todd he intended to have Mike retrieved within a few minutes because of security concerns. Todd asked if he could have a few more hours with Mike, but the governor declined. It was too dangerous to have him in a holding cell. There was too much at risk.

After the call ended, Todd relayed the information to Mike and told him he would visit him at his new location and promised that he would get fair treatment because he had been answering his questions. Mike seemed to be very nervous about this situation.

Within minutes, the sentinels arrived to retrieve him. The ambassador and Liz happened to be walking past and saw what was happening, so they stopped to watch Mike being loaded into the shielded container. The beige container was large enough for him to stand and was closed on three sides with a force field in front. Once he was inside, the container levitated and was easy to move. This was the same type of box in which Greg had been held.

Yalan heard the commotion and looked to see what was going on. Once she saw that Mike was being moved out of the complex, she moved closer in order to say goodbye. When she caught his glance, Mike quickly turned away. He was ashamed to be taken away like this in front of her because he truly liked Yalan. He wished things could be different, but he had always known that the path he had chosen would never allow them to be together.

As the sentinels started guiding Mike's container out of the room, Todd heard a static sound which grew louder and louder, until he saw what looked like a vertical crack with light protruding from it on all sides directly in the center of the room. A few seconds later, a haggard-looking Pertakian stepped out of the crack. He wasn't holding a weapon when he appeared, but because everyone watching was so shocked by what they were seeing, he got the jump on Todd and took his enforcer.

He pointed the enforcer outward and turned 360 degrees apparently attempting to get a bearing on who and what was around him. By now, everyone in the room was motionless, waiting for the assailant's next move. The Pertakian motioned with his newly acquired enforcer for the sentinels to step away from the hovering container which held Mike.

Once clear, he grabbed the container and moved it toward the crack which was still keeping its form in the center of the room. Still holding the enforcer out in a threatening manner, he pushed the container through the crack and followed it. Before exiting completely, he saw Liz and thought to himself, I'm going to finish the job that I started. Fenoc opened fire on Liz, hitting her with two short bursts. She fell back into her father's arms and slowly slumped to the floor. Within a few seconds, Fenoc dropped Todd's enforcer, slipped back through the crack, and disappeared.

For several moments, the group stood there in shocked silence. William Taylor sat down behind his daughter and held her in his arms. Uncharacteristically for the Ambassador, his confident demeanor disappeared, and he began to sob.

With a hollow feeling in his stomach, Todd motioned for the sentinels to come and collect his enforcer for analysis. Todd looked over at the ambassador, then looked down. He couldn't bear to see the sorrow in the father's eyes. He swore to himself that this incident wouldn't end here. No matter how long it took or what it cost him, Todd would find the ones responsible for this atrocity and bring them to justice, even if it meant going to the ends of PERTAK.